I0595938

THE STARTRAIL

-PORTAL PAINTER-

H. A. STEPHEN

Typography by E-book Formatting Fairies

FANTASTICAL PUBLISHING
Cover Design by Alexandra Purtan at
www.fenix-designs.com

For my true love, Alexander III.
And for my mom and dad, Wendy & Willard, the best encouragers
a daughter could have.

CHAPTER 1

The pool in the center of the room was sparkling with seafaen. Viggo knew this, he was the one that had to change the filters within it every month. The pool with seafaen that Panveer swam in to keep himself youthful, the pool amongst other pools in Ordillaz that affected the air all around them. Viggo got the job through a friend that he met after the war. He was a gardener named Jacobs who was connected to the landscapers that worked for Panveer, the most influential and powerful man in the Startrail and every realm within it. Powerful because he was the son of Ashook, who had taken control of the Startrail ten years ago. Ashook had limited the power of the Portal Painters, collaborating with Esmerelda, the most powerful Portal Painter in the Startrail. Rumor had it that it was the book, *The Esmerelda Letters,* that had persuaded the masses to follow anything that Ashook suggested. If Esmerelda now followed the Ashook movement, then why wouldn't everyone else?

Viggo looked around the room carefully, his eyes absorbing all that he could take in. It was only once a month that he came in to change the filters in the pool, so each time he tried to make the most of it. Panveer wasn't in his room. He was already changed and about to walk out onto the stage to give an important speech. There were only a few times he had ever been in the room at the same time as Panveer. Only once did Panveer look Viggo in the eye, catching Viggo off guard, because he tried to never look directly at him. Panveer didn't know who Viggo was, who he *really* was. That he was and would always be a true Erleonian at heart. He was determined that he would never know. For now, Viggo worked for this man, Panveer, whose father had destroyed his livelihood of mixing seafaen paint for the local Portal Painters. Now it didn't really matter, since everyone he once knew was dispersed, and no one had access to seafaen. The time of the Portal Painters had been over for ten years now. Any Portal Painter who might still exist was in hiding, and those who were known had been captured, killed, or used as servants of Ashook and now Panveer. They were at his bidding to create worlds for his new Startrail, one without Erleon. Esmerelda had painted new worlds for Ashook, worlds that he described as magnificent, but that others whispered were evil. Then Ashook had disappeared. Panveer had never revealed to the public where he went. Many believed he was dead, but others said he was living in one of the new worlds that were full of all he could ever want. Seafaen.

And loneliness, Viggo thought to himself.

He could still be out there in one of them, leaving his son in charge until the right time for his return.

Viggo put his hand in the water to scoop out some of it into his sieve. It would drain out the water but keep the seafaen. He knew this meant death. Or banishment from the realm. He knew it, but he didn't care. He needed to collect as much seafaen as he could, while he could. A part of him wanted to keep his hand in the pool, it felt so relieving to be in stardust-soaked water like that. It's how it always was meant to be, every realm saturated in stardust, the life-giving substance that made the Startrail connect. A substance that originated from Erleon, the birthplace of all realms, the realm that could never be lost, the realm that could never be seen. But now the seafaen was controlled in Ordillaz by Panveer and his United Ones. Just as they controlled access to the sacred Painter's Keep, where the seafaen flows from waterfalls.

He stood up quickly and wiped his hands on his pants. Two agents waltzed in with concerned looks on their faces. "Are you done in here?"

"Yes. The new filter is in." He tried to act natural while the agents slowly walked toward him. His hand felt like stone wrapped around his special bag full of seafaen. His heart pounded but he played it cool, as he did every month. The men continued to walk by him, their eyes watching Viggo move towards the doorway into the hall. Viggo's heart felt as though it would leap through his chest. Their eyes were black, a signature of all Panveer's agents, signifying their training level and the amount of stardust they ingested daily. A rationed amount that only those privileged in Ordillaz Realm could consume. Viggo hated it. Stardust wasn't supposed to be ingested as a drink; it was supposed to be lived in and felt. This was the way of Ashook and his son, it was partly what made their regime so attractive to some.

Finally, he was outside and in the hall. Every month it was a risk for him to collect the seafaen, but this was why he valued his job, why he stayed put as a laborer, because these few moments every month were precious to him.

Purposeful.

As he left the room, footsteps could be heard behind him. Viggo didn't look back, he had to play it cool.

"Excuse me." One of the agents' voices echoed in the hall.

Viggo turned around slowly, nerves in his mouth. Most months he didn't run into any of the agents, but he'd been noticing an increase in security as of late.

Please don't get caught, he told himself.

"You left your tools," one agent said.

Viggo tried to remain calm. The agent was two feet away from him. They had sensors for seafaen but the sieve that he had was strong in hiding what was within. He left the sieve in his jacket pocket and reached out to take the tools. The agent was tall and loomed over him, his black eyes like tar staring into his soul.

"Don't be so forgetful next time," the agent growled.

The other agent was standing behind him. He piped up, "I don't know why he doesn't get one of us to change the filters, it's probably easy enough."

Once Viggo took his tools, the agents backed away and turned to walk down the hall. Viggo waited until they left, as was custom. Always wait until an agent of Panveer walks away first, then that is your permission to leave.

Relief set over him; he had what he needed with minimal questioning. He wondered how long it would last—the agents were right, it was an easy job. He felt favored that the job had been given to him, which was why he made sure to make the most of each opportunity.

He had to get back to Marigold and Jewel. If they could all travel out of Ordillaz tonight, they would. Viggo had one portal painting in his keeping that had been given to him by his close friend. It was hiding deep underground, underneath his home. He knew that, after today, he finally had enough seafaen to make a trip through the portal to another realm— but only for one person. He also had an extra amount for emergencies. Or if he were to ever cross paths with a Portal Painter again, he would happily give up what he had for them to use.

He had to get out of the palace quarters quickly, but he was too close to the Painter's Turret. Every month there was the same dilemma, to stop at the turret or continue. He always stopped. It was up the winding stairs and nestled at the top. That was where the Painters who worked for Panveer were required to be stationed. At least, that was what the common thought was. No one had actually seen a Portal Painter for a long time, only those who worked for them and created the seafaen paint for them to use. He walked up the stairs swiftly, looking behind on occasion to ensure he wasn't being watched. Once he was at the top of the stairs, he didn't dare to open the door. There were alarms and diamond-seers within rooms like that. The diamond-seers were diamonds that allowed Panveer, or whoever wanted to know, to see what was going on in the room.

Viggo stood outside, as he usually did on his monthly trips to the pools. He stood outside hoping the door would someday open. Hoping he would hear something. As times before, there was no sound, nothing happened. He closed his eyes and waited for one more minute, longer than he usually did. Still nothing happened. Disappointed, he slowly walked back down the stairs. Knowing that the Portal Painters were within the turret, just steps away, was enough to stir hope within him. *They exist, they always have, they always will*, he said to himself.

Suddenly, the door opened a few stairs above him. Surprised, he started to run down the stairs, hoping no one would hear him. He paused in the shadows. No one was coming downstairs, but voices could be heard.

"Stop it." An urgent whisper was heard.

"I can't work here anymore, now that I know that," a voice moaned tearfully.

"There's nothing to know, Keltie."

Viggo continued to shuffle forward and down the stairs.

He needed to get out of the stairwell, lest anyone saw him and became suspicious.

Keltie's voice was muffled with tears. "How would the keys be missing? We're doomed. Our jobs are finished here. Who knows what they will do to us?"

"Calm down, Keltie," the other woman reprimanded.

"There's strange powers that they have access to. I heard that servants have been turned into stone. Statues for the gardens." Keltie's voice was frantic.

"We don't know the facts. Just because we are unable to access the Painter's Keep this time doesn't mean …" The voice was harder to hear. "It doesn't mean the keys went missing. How could they? Don't you know the security that surrounds them?"

"You don't suppose that *she* …" Keltie's voice faltered. Keltie was backing down the steps slowly.

"That *she* could be alive?" The other woman's voice cut her off. "Adrian was just bluffing. She died in the war, the only thing that is left from her are the letters."

The Esmerelda Letters, Viggo reflected. They were talking about Esmerelda. He felt as though his ears grew two sizes making the effort to listen.

"If she was alive, how would it matter?" the stern woman continued.

"I have heard rumors, people saying that it's Esmerelda who controls the access point to the Painter's Keep," Keltie added.

"Who told you that?" The other woman's voice was angry and mocking. "Portal Painters don't have that much power, Keltie. It's those who help guide their ministries who hold the power."

"I know, I know," Keltie whispered, voice shaking.

Viggo felt the heat rise up within him. He wished he could

rush up there and defend the Portal Painters, but he refrained. It was beyond him how the lies about the Startrail could have gone as far as they had, how *The Esmerelda Letters* had carried such a following. He knew Esmerelda. Her character was never questionable, she would never disown Erleon, she would never write against Portal Painters' powers. He could never understand why she was so loyal to Ashook. But no one could ever know. Ashook had created a secret society that it was almost impossible to be a part of, and once the people caught wind that Esmerelda was supportive of it, Ashook's popularity soared. The Ashook Wars were ten years ago, and Esmerelda hadn't been seen since.

Viggo was able to get to the ground level and into the main hall quietly. He picked up the pace. He was already five minutes past his usual schedule for being in the inner courts, which was where the speech took place. Severe punishment was in store for those who were off schedule—that is, if caught by an agent. If a staff member was not in the right place at the right time, they were questioned, banished from the realm, or put to death.

He made it to the inner courts, six minutes late, without being caught. A voice could be heard outside, echoing over the crowds. Panveer was already midway into his speech preparing Ordillaz Realm for a huge infrastructure expansion. Viggo walked past the back door to the stage and walked along the perimeter of the crowds.

The keys are missing, keys to the Painter's Keep. He couldn't believe what he had just overheard, the weight of it all. If he knew Erleonian lore, and he did, then that would mean that the Portal Painter in power had released the keys to the next Portal Painter. That would mean Esmerelda is alive. Or, maybe the keys were stolen or had gone missing—there was no way to know for sure. He reflected on all that he had heard from Keltie and the other woman before directing his attention to Panveer.

Panveer's voice boomed into the crowd. "What if I told you that we were two worlds away from sustainability without Erleonian roots? Roots that uphold the Portal Painters like gods while forgetting about the rest of us. Regular people like you. Like me." He paused and looked out to the crowd.

"The realms may be few, but we can continue to uphold the new message of the Portal Painter Esmerelda who made it her mission to show that Painters are powerful in and of themselves, and so is everyone else. It is not about some foreign realm that we cannot even see on the map. It's been a decade since the era of the Portal Painters and now we step even more confidently into a new era, one that will focus on a few realms and build them into powerful and dominant worlds, full of beauty and imagination."

Viggo walked past what seemed to be thousands of people gathered in the large courtyard in the center of Geth, Ordillaz. *Blind followers*, he thought. He leaned against a stone wall.

"Why does he have to speak so eloquently?" A golden-haired young woman joined Viggo against the wall. "Hi Dad." She looked at her father, who was watching all the people's hopeful eyes staring up at Panveer. She was wearing a black fur hat and a long jacket. The air was much colder in the evening.

"What are you doing out here so late?"

"I thought I was supposed to meet you here?"

"Not right down at the courts." Viggo knew he was being irrational. His daughter, Jewel, and his wife, Marigold, would often meet him after work and walk home with him. "He spews out lies so handsomely." Viggo's neck flexed. He looked away from the stage.

Panveer was building up his following now that he had decided to settle in Ordillaz, a world once dominated by his father, Ashook. Ashook was the prince of Ordillaz, son of a successful Portal Painter, Devra, and her husband and protector, Jatro. Devra had painted the realm of Ordillaz herself and it was considered to be one of the most unique and beautiful worlds ever created. Jatro and Devra reigned during the time when Portal Painters roamed free. Realm to realm they would travel, creating new worlds whenever they wished. New worlds that would come with new populations and fully formed rules, culture, and rhythms. Sadly, many of these worlds had been destroyed during the Ashook Wars; the amount of loss was insurmountable.

Ashook knew Portal Painters well, but he himself didn't have the gift, and neither did his son.

The gift comes to those with the heart for it, who have Erleon in their blood. Viggo considered this as they walked past a group of young men chatting about Panveer's speech.

"It would solve all the issues. We could have an even flow of seafaen, just like it is in the fabled Painter's Keep!" one man piped up, leaning against a stone wall that jutted up high above him, just one of the walls within the maze-like city of Geth, the heart of Ordillaz.

"Fabled keep? If only these people knew how real that place is," Viggo said under his breath to his daughter. His fists stiffened.

"Sounds like he's just trying to be generous." Another man joined the conversation. "Is he really going to make that happen? Stardust brings about more stardust. If there's no birthplace, then there's no seafaen for anyone."

"Are you talking about the fictional birthplace of the Startrail? Erleon? You can't believe that," the first man scoffed back.

"I believe that Portal Painters must have received their gift from somewhere," the second man argued.

"It's a gift that comes randomly, it's within a person. It's not from a place. No one can even see it on the star map," the other man spewed.

"It doesn't mean it isn't there," the second man replied.

"You better watch what you say around these parts, Mick. That way of thinking is gone, it's from another era. We are growing as a realm now, you have to see that."

Viggo wished he could join in; he wanted to pat Mick on the back. He was being brave. Geth was becoming like many of the other cities within the realms of the Startrail; it wasn't giving significance to Erleon or to the Portal Painters. It was turning its back on the true functioning of the Startrail and trying to come up with its own way of bringing in necessary stardust. It was trying to control the power of the seafaen.

"How can people think that the Portal Painters shouldn't be free? What happened to imagination and the beauty of art? What happened to freedom and bringing life?" Viggo's golden-haired daughter whispered.

"It's because of this." He reached into his pocket and pulled out a small leather bag. He knew that Jewel knew what it was. "It's currency."

"Dad, keep that away."

They weren't allowed to carry seafaen around, not freely, since the Ashook Wars happened ten years ago.

"Let's get out of here. Your mother is waiting for us at the tree," Viggo said.

"Dad, what if someone follows us? What if they know who you are?" Jewel asked, worry pooled in her eyes.

He placed his hand on his chest. The mark of Erleon was under his sweater. Jewel watched carefully. "My role in the wars is old news. Look at me now, with all my friends scattered. All who I fought along with are gone. They wouldn't care about me right now."

"If they knew about what you've been up to …" she continued.

"They won't know, I promise. Your brother is being trained up so that when it is time, our family will be ready." He paused and looked out at the dark road ahead of them. "Ready for when the Portal Painters take control of the Painter's Keep again. We are doing all that we can, we just have to play the part for a little longer—until I get enough seafaen for us all to leave this place."

He looked at Jewel and motioned for her to move along. They walked through a dark alley, leaving the crowds behind. The dark alley led to a semi-lit courtyard, people's homes and windows were within the walls next to them. Jewel looked down. Being part of the resistance group that protected Painters from Ashook's initiatives meant that they had to be secretive about where they went. Now, they were on the outskirts of the city, where the giant trees were. Their home was in one of them. The lights were illuminated within.

Ivo, Viggo's eldest son, had grown up with powers gifted from Erleon—not portal painting powers, but he had a natural gift of homing in on the power of the stardust that was natural in each realm and wielding it to do his own bidding. Marigold and Viggo saw that Ivo had this gift and sent him off for training to a hidden Portal Forest within a realm so limited in stardust it really made no sense for them to send him there. And this is why they did so. They sent him to Earth Realm because they assumed that Panveer would not care to inspect this realm, not like the other five surviving realms. Viggo's heart sank at the thought of there only being six realms now, when there used to be millions before the Ashook Wars.

Marigold met them at the door to their tree.

"We've heard the news about Ordillaz growing. We are going to need to leave soon. They … they are thinking of evacuating Earth Realm." Tears in her eyes, she looked at Jewel and back at Viggo.

Viggo pulled Marigold into his arms. They stood in the doorway for a moment and he reached out for Jewel. "It's going to be OK. He isn't going to do what Ashook did."

"He couldn't." Marigold's voice shook.

"No, he really won't." Viggo looked into their eyes.

"Why is that? How do you know?"

"They wouldn't destroy any portals if there's a chance that something precious is within them."

They looked at him questioningly.

"I think the keys are missing, and I may be one of the first to know."

CHAPTER 2

It was something she thought everyone must have memories of, and yet she couldn't pinpoint exactly what the memory was about or where it came from. Was it of birth? All she could recall was emerging from a place and entering a new world. It was like going through a portal. Flashes of color, starry skies, a glimpse of someone watching, eyes looking, seeing, and then finally, deep blue darkness, this is what she could remember. It was a memory that felt cold and distant, yet familiar and like home. Sarah Carlson looked back in her journal from six years ago. The entry was from her last years of elementary school, and that memory kept shooting back into her brain like an asteroid falling and crashing into the earth. But it was all so faint, like a dream that kept escaping her, just like all her memories before the age of seven. That was why this memory stuck to her like superglue. It was a twinkle of hope. The only memory that she had from before. She read it out to herself: "Lights, soft lights and darkness, cold black earth. I felt the warmth of the sun, but it wasn't the sun, it was sparkling like the stars in the sky. A blanket covered me. Flashing like lightning, the color whirling around."

She held on to that journal entry like a keepsake from her forgotten past, a past that she desperately wanted to know. She thought about painting the memory and considered the colors that she'd use. It's no use, she thought to herself. Tears began to pour out of her eyes. Her father hadn't shown up to the art show at school. Her own art show. Sarah was the only student selected for this honor. There were other artists—singers, dancers and fashion designers—showcasing what they had designed and prepared. But Sarah was the only painter. Her teacher told her that she had a gift, a gift beyond what she had ever seen. Every splash of encouragement only led to a heart-sinking recognition that her dad wouldn't change, or ever understand her love for art and painting. It was a heavy burden to bear over all these years since the accident. Deep down, she had known that he wouldn't be there for the art show. But there was that small ounce of hope that she had, that this one time, he would come around and things would be different.

She stormed in after the show was over and ran up to her room, not facing her dad. She was disappointed and frustrated. Let down again and again, her journal was her comfort. It brought a certain stability that no human could give her. Within, it held a piece of what happened before. A distant memory that held personal meaning for her. Sarah wiped her tears on her sweater sleeve and placed the journal on her desk, then sat down on the chair in front of it, facing the large window where what was left of the evening light streamed through.

She remembered two years ago when he took her paints and easel and threw them outside into the rain puddles in the backyard. Sarah remembered seeing hurt in his eyes. She hadn't made an effort to paint at home since that day.

"Extra grace required," her grandfather would say when it came to her dad, but this one hurt. It wasn't his fault, though. How could Sarah blame him? He dealt with migraines and blackouts due to amnesia from the accident that happened ten years ago. Ever since she could remember, he had been on medication that would keep him from dangerous blackouts and the heavy migraines. He was told to take the medication every day to keep these painful side effects at bay. They were lucky to be alive; the news reports described the accident as a head-on collision. Sarah's dad was unconscious and in a coma for a few days. Sarah suffered a serious concussion and had also dealt with migraines ever since. She was so young, only seven at the time. They both lost memories that made them who they were, but it affected her father more, since there was more to lose for him. Thankfully, her grandfather helped make sense of what had happened and who they were and, ultimately, who they were supposed to be. Sarah sat quietly in front of the window overlooking her favorite forest of trails. If she couldn't paint, she would doodle and draw. She pushed away the anger, the sadness, and tried to zone out.

Just then, she saw it. Something sparkled in the group of evergreens in the forest outside her window, a slight illumination between the trees, as if the northern lights dipped low and laced themselves around the branches. It was a strange thing to see anywhere, let alone a forest, but this was a normal sight for Sarah. She had walked up to the sparkle many times before and dipped her hand into it. It didn't feel like anything, but it left a light sheen on her hand that disappeared after a while. There was a time when she thought that everyone could see it. She tried to show it to her best friend Stina, but Stina couldn't see anything at all. Stina's response — "You've got an amazing imagination, my friend"— marched back into her mind every time she saw the lights.

Imagination. It was too real to be just that. When she first saw the lights, she was a small child, maybe eight or nine, and she remembered running back to her father and shouting for him to come and see. But he couldn't confirm her sightings. Sarah could tell that he was trying. When she dragged him out to the forest to show him again and again, he began to get worried and made her get her eyes checked and see a psychologist. Her dad would say it was, once again, because of the accident those many years ago that Sarah began "seeing things." Sarah began to ignore what she saw and accept it as something that she needed to keep to herself.

They were more pronounced today as she sat in front of her journal at her desk. It was almost as if the lights were waving at her, calling out to her, but she had learned to brush off thoughts that she deemed to be "crazy." Her eyes locked onto the trees. The evening sky landed softly over top of them and the lights spun around each tree.

"Ugh, I hate this!" She stood up at her desk and pulled down the blind on the window. *No one understands. Why do I see that stuff? Why?* she questioned herself. Sarah was tired of the confusion and how it made her migraines start up. The blind shot up on its own. Sarah gasped. She pulled it down again, but it was like a heavy weight and wouldn't come down. She left it open and her eyes again locked onto the lights in the trees. The darkness of the evening sky allowed for the stars to be seen. Sarah squinted her eyes and moved closer to the window. The stars looked like they were all gathered above the forest for a split second, and then they scattered. The whirling glow of the lights around the trees spun faster and then started to move away from the trees and toward the house. Her migraine began; she closed her eyes, and begged the pain to go away.

Draw something.

She heard a voice in her mind which startled her. She could swear that she heard the words audibly.

Draw something.

It was her own voice, she assumed. She looked around the room. It was darkened now, her journal was open to a blank sheet of paper. The sparkles from the forest were flowing like a trail, up to her window. Sarah focused on the trail, it flowed through her window and wrapped around her pencil. Sarah stepped back.

Draw something.

She closed her eyes. Many times in the past, when she would see strange things or when headaches and migraines would start, she would close her eyes and breathe. When she opened her eyes, they would be gone. But this time, it was more invasive, the lights came right into her room.

"What … what is this?" She looked around carefully. "Stop it!"

She heard shuffling from her dad downstairs. "Sarah, are you OK?"

"Yeah! I'm OK," she said quickly. She had learned to ignore it, to keep quiet about all the strange things she saw.

She kept her eyes closed and sat on the chair in front of the desk and breathed. When she opened them, she was in another room. It wasn't real, but it felt real. Was she in a memory? A vision? A dream? Maybe she had fallen asleep. She felt like she was standing on air, but she was in a room. It was like she was being taken back, forced to recall something, something that she didn't recall before. In this place, Sarah was feeling so homesick for her father. She was taken back to that first year after the accident, when he was away at rehab and her grandfather raised her. Tears were in her eyes, she remembered now. Someone at school made fun of her for not having a mother. Sarah felt the pain of brokenness that her little self experienced that day. Why had she forgotten it until now? She wanted to ask her grandfather about her mom. She was sneaking into one of her grandfather's meetings that he held on occasion at her house. She was never allowed to be in the meetings. A strange man was standing in front of her grandfather and holding out his hand. In his hand there was a flipped over locket that revealed a symbol. A ruby gem sparkled on the other side of the locket.

The symbol on the necklace was of keys, three of them, each pointing in different directions. Sarah was seeing this in front of her. It was like she saw it with her own eyes, but she was back when she was only seven. It felt like slow motion, but she moved her head to the right and she saw a painting on the office desk. It was bright and looked like it was moving. Colors were swirling around. As soon as Sarah entered the room, the strange man started shouting at her grandfather to get her out of the room. His yelling clanked against her mind. She remembered the man covering the painting up with a sheet.

The voice spoke again, *portal painting.*

"I want my mom. Where is she?" her brave self asked.

"What is this?" the strange man asked, anger on his face. It was blurry, but he was obviously upset.

"She doesn't know, she doesn't get it," her grandfather tried to explain. He promptly took Sarah by the hand and left her outside the door with no explanation.

Draw something.

The voice, her voice, reminded.

The vision or whatever it was ended. She opened her eyes again and saw her desk, the stream of lights wrapped around her pencil was still there.

"What just happened?" she whispered. It was the first time she had really thought back to that time when she went to see Grandfather in his office. But she remembered it now.

She felt scared. It was a weird experience and what she saw wasn't relevant to her back then. But now it stood out. It was like a veil had been lifted.

All the reasons for her mother leaving flooded back. The reality that she knew from her past was from Grandfather. It provided stability. Reasons.

Her mother was a drug addict, she used her family for her own gain, then she took off, never to be seen again.

"Foolish," Grandfather told her dad one time. "You're foolish to have married her."

It felt like Sarah's background and history were like puzzle pieces trying to fit back into the picture. But why, why now? Why the lights? Why were they in the room?

She picked up the pencil that was laced with the lights and drew what came to mind, the keys pointing in different directions, the ones on the necklace that the strange man in Grandfather's office was talking about. She shaded in one of the keys on the page. The exact shape of them, she couldn't quite remember, but as she drew, her headache started up again. She closed her eyes tight and then opened them and looked at the page. Her drawings became more prominent in detail as she drew, they seemed to come alive. The three keys almost jumped off the page. Sarah leaned back against her chair. She felt equally satisfied and conflicted about what she had just drawn, but once again, she ignored it all and closed up the journal. She would have to face her father eventually. She knew that he would be feeling bad about the art show. Her plan was to tell her dad about going to art school after she graduated, but she knew he wouldn't be in the mood, especially today. Her heart sank and tears pricked the back of her eyes. She took a deep breath and swallowed up her sadness.

Sarah started down the creaky wooden steps, clinging to her journal with the writings and drawings in it. She knew her father was trying to make amends after missing her art show at school. She could smell homemade pizza cooking in the oven. Her dad felt guilty, she could tell, but she just couldn't hold anything against him. The amnesia was at fault and she hated it. It wasn't fair that her dad had to go through all this mental agony. She looked around the dining room and then sat down on one of the chairs.

"Should be another ten minutes before the pizza's ready," Sarah's dad, Stanley, said. He looked at her, as if he wanted to say something else, but hesitated.

Sarah said, "Dad? It's okay about the show. I know it bothers you that I paint and it's fine. But I wanted to show you something that I drew. Drawing is OK, right?"

"I don't know why it is that I am this way. I … I am sorry that I missed your show." He looked down. "This is my way of apologizing. I know I haven't been the father you deserve."

He looked over at Sarah's journal which was laid out on the table, she flipped it to the page with her drawings on it.

He cleared his throat and moved forward, looking down at the three keys.

"Interesting," her father said. He looked at the picture with concern in his eyes.

"I was just reminded of something, a memory that I had," Sarah said. She was eager to share her experience, like it was a revelation that would help them both put the pieces of their past back together. "It just came to me, like, all of a sudden. It was like I woke up and remembered." Her dad looked at her with worried eyes. She continued, "I snuck into Grandpa's office. He was having a meeting there and it was when you were at rehab. Some man gave Grandfather a necklace. It had this symbol on it, the one I tried to draw here. There also was a …" She didn't know if she should mention the painting, but she braved it out. "A painting. It was sparkling and seemed to be moving, like it was alive."

Her dad blinked heavily and shook his head slowly. "I don't remember any special meetings that he would have. That year while I was in rehab, that must have been hard for you. I don't think we ever really talked about it." He stepped back from the drawings.

"I was homesick for you, a lot," Sarah said. "I know it's a strange memory to have. I mean, maybe it wasn't a memory. A moving painting seems crazy, it must have been in my imagination. I saw the lights again, upstairs just now, in the forest, and the memory just shot out at me. I don't know why I didn't remember it before."

Her father didn't reply.

"I know," Sarah said quietly. "I know you don't like hearing about the lights and all that crazy stuff. But it was more intense this time, Dad. Like … like … something was trying to …"

"Sarah," Stanley interrupted in a stern whisper. "The accident has left you with your own burdens to bear. It's not uncommon for you to see the shimmering lights in the trees and the like."

Sarah recalled all the times she tried to get her dad to see what she saw, with no success.

"The whirling colors that you saw in the …" She knew he didn't want to say "painting."

"In the painting?" Sarah finished his sentence.

He cleared his throat and closed his eyes, opening them again slowly like they were made of heavy bricks. "It's an illusion, Sarah, something you need to ignore."

"But it was just so strange and felt so real. I don't know why it suddenly came to me. It almost felt like a vision," she continued.

Her father didn't respond.

Sarah moved into the living room and sat on the couch, leaving her opened journal on the dining room table. She wished that she hadn't said anything, but she was proud of what she had drawn and hoped it would help bring up the topic of art school. There was movement at the door. Grandfather entered in a hurry, as hurried as he could be using his walker. Sarah noticed him looking around frantically, searching for something.

"Grandfather?"

He looked at Sarah and then walked up to Stanley.

"Dad. Did the nurses drive you?"

Grandfather was catching his breath.

"What's going on?" Stanley asked. "Sit down, Dad."

He didn't sit down. "I just needed to see if you guys …" He looked at Sarah. "Have you guys noticed anything strange around the house lately? You didn't find anything unusual or strange, did you? Anything lying around?" He was still frantically looking around.

Sarah shook her head. "No. What are you talking about?" She thought of the strange lights and the random experience that she had as she was drawing, but she knew that sharing that wouldn't mean anything.

He shot his hands up. "OK, that's all I need to know."

"What kind of strange stuff?" Sarah asked.

"Dad, what exactly are you looking for? Should we be expecting something to be delivered here?" Stanley asked.

"It's too hard to explain at the moment," Grandfather said. "But here I am, now." He looked around. "What's for dinner?"

He walked over to Sarah, saw her journal on the table and looked at the picture. He looked up into her eyes carefully. "Did you draw that?" He lifted the journal close to his eyes and then slowly placed it back on the table. "Where did you come up with that?" His wrinkled finger was directly on top of the keys that she had drawn.

She supposed it was her chance to ask him about the new memory that she had just recalled.

"Since I haven't been able to paint much, I thought it would be okay to draw."

"The picture. Why did you draw *this* picture?" her grandfather asked. His tone was stern.

"Well, it was a memory I had. At least I think it was." She could tell her grandfather wasn't happy. It's just a stupid memory, she told herself. It wouldn't matter if she shared it—he would ignore it anyway. "I came into your office and …" she paused. Her grandfather's eyes pierced hers. She felt uncertain if she should continue. "And … someone was giving you a necklace. A necklace with this symbol on it."

He mumbled something to himself.

Sarah continued, "It was just something that I remembered tonight, that's all. I don't know why I didn't think of it before."

"Tonight? You remembered all that tonight?" He looked at his watch and furrowed his brow. "You aren't supposed to remember." He looked around and mumbled something to himself again. He looked into her eyes, "What else do you remember?"

"But the thing is, I don't think it happened before the accident," Sarah said. She was watching her grandfather's face carefully, trying to think of why he was so frantic.

"What else do you remember?" he pressed on.

"Well, this part is just crazy, but there was a painting. It was … it was moving around, whirling about," Sarah continued.

"Painting," Grandfather whispered. "You remember that, suddenly. Out of the blue, you remembered something like that."

"What do you think it was? How could a painting move like that?" she asked. "It's silly, I know."

"I think it's the amnesia, it's the collision. It's always made you see things, strange things." He was abrupt and careless with his words. "Forget it, altogether."

"What do you mean?" Sarah probed her grandfather. "Why did you ask me about it, then?"

"You know what? Forget dinner too. I really should be on my way. The staff from the seniors' home are waiting to drive me back."

"You just got here," Stanley said. "What is going on, Dad?"

"Grandfather, please," Sarah added.

Grandfather continued toward the door. "I need to take care of some things. Now."

"What's going on, Dad? Why did you rush over here?" Stanley tried to get more answers.

"It's too hard to explain, Stanley. Just know that I am …" He cleared his throat and looked around. "I'm sorry that it has to be this way. Believe me, I am. Things may be a bit"—he looked around, subtle emotion entered his voice—"different from now on."

Stanley looked confused. "What are you talking about?" He tried to help his father out the door, but his father brushed him away with his hand. "Just tell me what you mean!"

Grandfather paused halfway out the door and looked back.

"Did you find anything, Sarah? Anything strange, anything at all?" he asked, as if everything awaited Sarah's answer. "Please tell me." His eyes looked into hers. "I know it's strange that I'm asking this, but you make sure you tell me. If you find anything."

She felt at a loss for words. "I don't know what you are wanting me to say."

He impatiently continued out the door.

The pizza timer went off in the kitchen and Stanley rushed toward it. Sarah stayed by the window and watched a staff member meet her grandfather and take him to the vehicle. The vehicle was parked a few yards away from the house and Sarah noticed that it wasn't the same seniors' home community van that he usually used. Instead, a door to a black limo opened and a woman who Sarah had never seen before helped him in. She had long white hair, but the details of her face couldn't be seen.

"Weird," Sarah said. "The seniors' home got a major upgrade."

"How so?" her dad asked from the dining room.

"They use limos now?" Sarah said. "Grandpa just drove off in a black limo."

"What? Really?" Stanley walked to the window, but the car had already driven away. "That's strange. I don't know what's gotten into him."

"Why did he say that I wasn't supposed to remember that? I told him that the memory wasn't from before the accident," Sarah said. "He was so upset about my drawing."

"I think we both know that your grandfather is having his own amount of memory loss. I think he's just having an off day. I'll give him a call later and see what that was all about. Looks like he's being taken care of quite well over there, with the limo and all."

They both laughed.

"I always thought that any new memory we had could be information that would help us." Sarah's voice faltered.

"Grandfather won't understand that. He's trying to protect us. It's been ten years, and now … now were used to this, this life we have. Simple. Easy." Sarah could tell that he wasn't convinced. "He doesn't want us scraping up any memories that may or may not be accurate. He wants us to move on."

They sat in the dining room without talking for a few minutes before Sarah brought up her sketches once again.

She wanted to ask him about art school, the application had to be in within a couple of days.

"Dad, I feel that I am good enough—good enough to maybe go to art school. Once I graduate." She held out the sketches once again.

"Sarah, I don't think we can talk about this right now. I …" He closed his eyes and rubbed his head.

"But Dad, I was hoping that tonight we could really talk about why it is that you won't let me"—she searched in vain for another way to say it—"paint."

He stood up and walked towards the entrance to the dining room.

She continued, "I need to apply by Friday. Why don't you like the idea of art school?"

She followed him. "Look! I drew these. And I can paint them too. Painting isn't going to harm you, nothing will hurt you, Dad!" Tears were behind her eyes, the anger from him missing her art show was coming to the surface. "I feel like you don't care. You are keeping me from my dreams because of some hang-up you have."

She could tell her dad was trying hard to look at the sketch book. He breathed deep and clenched his fist. "It is not a hang-up." He put his hand on his forehead. "You know it bothers me. You know it bothers me. So, why, why must we keep talking about it?"

Sarah could tell he was feeling pain in his head.

"I know, I know." She was trying to be sensitive. "I'm sorry. But why painting? Something must have happened before the accident. Something that had to do with it? Maybe your body is just remembering somehow."

He sat down abruptly on the chair. "It's best to not talk about it."

"But maybe we can figure this out."

"Enough!" He shot back out of the chair and breathed

heavily. Sarah was taken aback. Her father didn't lash out in anger very often. He paused, his eyes closed, warding off the headache. "I'll go get the pizza."

Her father went into the kitchen, ignoring the sketch-book. A few moments went by and then she heard a huge crash.

"Dad?" When he didn't respond, Sarah rushed into the kitchen. Her journal and drawings fell to the floor, the picture of the three keys twinkled in the evening light.

Her heart dropped. She hoped it wasn't another episode. "Dad, not again!"

But there he was, flat out on the kitchen floor. Sarah dove down beside him and found his pulse and could see that he was still breathing.

Another blackout meant another trip to Emergency. She was used to it now. Sarah knew that it was because her father wasn't taking his medication daily. The medication that would ward off hallucinations, migraines and blackouts, not to mention the visions. He once told her that he liked to get the visions. They brought him information, he would say, information about his past. Sarah felt bad. How she longed for him to have his memories back. They both longed to know more about their past, more than just what Grandfather told them. They both continued to grasp onto whatever they could that would fill that void. The void that echoed the question back at them, *is there more? Is there more to know?*

CHAPTER 3

The sky was clouding over, evening approached, and the shadows tucked in their small two- story home in the suburbs for the night. Sarah's home sat on the end of a cul-de-sac which included four other homes. A large forested area with ample trails edged the neighborhood. Her father was sitting in his usual chair in the living room, watching baseball again. A box of old photos sat in a shoebox by his chair. Sarah noticed that he was holding a picture of Grandfather, Sarah, and himself, out fishing. It was at a nearby lake and she must have been eight years old. He continued to stare at the picture as if he had never seen it before, then he'd look through some other pictures for a while and promptly go back to looking at the same one of them fishing. It had been a week since the blackout and trip to the hospital. Stanley was doing much better, but Sarah noticed that this was the third night in a row that he was looking at the one picture.

"We should really put those photos in an album," Sarah commented. They never had any albums of pictures, or any in frames, not like how her friends had them. Stina's family had shelves full of photo albums from when Stina and her brother were babies, all the way up. She supposed if she had a mother, her mother would do all those things for them. She would make their home warmer, more put together. Her dad just wasn't the kind of guy to go the extra mile in that way.

"Feel free," he smiled, and huffed, "Purchase an album and go for it!"

"OK, maybe on the weekend!" Sarah said. "Hey Dad, what exactly does grandfather do?"

"Well, he plays cards with his friends. He's at the seniors' home most of the time," he answered, still staring at the picture.

"Not now, but, like, before. His career. He still worked when I was little."

"An architect. He focused on new home builds. He was able to work from home, which helped our situation." He looked at Sarah briefly, and his eyes held a sadness, an exhaustion. "Why do you ask?"

"Just curious. I keep thinking about that memory I had, the meetings that he had."

"Well honey, I think the memory is best left alone. It really doesn't matter now, anyway."

Sarah wanted to keep asking more about her grandfather but decided against it. She put on her running shoes and light sweater. "I'm going for my run now. The one through the ravine, the half-hour loop."

"Did you finish your homework?" he felt obligated to ask. Sarah recognized that he felt more father-like when he asked questions like that.

"Yeah, Dad, it's done," Sarah laughed.

As soon as Sarah left the house, the rain started. Fall rains were cold and crisp and left her chilled to the bone by the end of her run. Her track team was doing base training, which meant a lot of cross-country. The canopying trees waved as she entered the trail, shielding her from the rain. The tree roots piled over one another into clusters while squirrels roamed around their small kingdoms. Her senses were always stirred in this place, and she continued to see the beautiful sparkling glow that laced the trees. She could always see the lights, but ever since last week, when she had the vision in her room and drew the picture of the keys, the glowing lights had been more prominent than before, way more apparent. They were so pronounced and beautiful that it caused her to stop in her tracks and look around. But if she looked too long at the sparkles, her headaches would start again. It was as if they set something off in her head. She closed her eyes and tried to shake off the ache.

Opening them again, she noticed the lights moving faster, quicker, like mini tornados. The tops of the trees swayed gently in the wind. The wind was heavy and rushed through like an ocean wave. The lights got brighter, making her shut her eyes. The headache burned in her head. When she opened her eyes, the strange substance that only she could see circled her hands and danced in front of her. Sarah collapsed to the ground and squeezed her eyes shut again as if to ward off the lights and the pain she felt in her head. She felt the sharpness of the jagged roots beneath her knees. When she opened her eyes again, she gasped. In front of her was a shining bright key. She looked around, assuming someone else would be there, but she was alone.

"What is this?" she whispered. Her head still hurt but she was distracted by the beautiful item that had just appeared before her. She picked it up but looked around again. Had someone dropped the key in front of her?

Sarah looked at her watch and noticed that she had been out for longer than half an hour. It was starting to get dark. She picked up the key and put it in the pocket of her sweater and zipped it up. When she got back to the entrance of the cul-de-sac, she looked back. The lights were still there, and they were getting brighter and more intense. It felt like her migraine was her very self, trying to rip open her memories. It felt like someone was trying to tell her something. But it was all too crazy, and she had to follow protocol, shake it off and ignore. Sarah took a deep breath and pulled out the key to look at it once more. It was so beautiful, like an antique, but it didn't look old or worn. It was golden with one jewel on the top of it. She put the key into her pocket again and turned her gaze toward her home. She noticed that the car was gone from the driveway; she quickened her step and hurried into the house.

"Dad?" she called out.

She walked in. The TV was still on, but her dad was nowhere to be found. Sarah considered that he might have gone to the store, but what would they have needed? He had stopped to get groceries on the way home from work.

He hadn't left a note. She decided to call him on his phone. No answer. Sarah went into the kitchen, poured herself a glass of water, and dried her rain-soaked hair with a towel. Walking back to the living room, she saw the shoebox that was left open near Dad's chair. The picture that he had been looking at wasn't in there, from what she could see. There were other ones, from old birthday parties, and more of Grandfather taking them on outings. And there were some Christmas cards in there, mostly from Grandfather, a few from Dad's work friends, and of course there were Sarah's handcrafted cards made for her dad for Father's Day. There were some nice mementos in that shoebox, but Sarah couldn't help but feel a little low. How sad was it that all their memories as a family fit in a little shoebox, and didn't even fill it all the way up? She placed the box back on the ground and looked out the window, hoping her father would pull up soon. All those memories, birthday parties, celebrations were what she knew, they were special to her, but they seemed so lacking when she started to compare her life to her friends' experiences. She felt bad comparing. Her dad did try to do his best for her. The rain was pouring down hard, Sarah was feeling uneasy. She locked the front door and pulled down the blinds.

She picked up the phone to call Stina.

"So, my dad just drove off, and didn't tell me where he is going."

Stina responded, "Yeah, so? You're worried? He'll be back! Are you sure you're not the dad?"

"It's just late, and we just got back from the hospital only a week ago, so, you know, I'm worried," Sarah added as she closed the curtains of the kitchen windows.

"Is it because it's raining and thundering out there?" Stina questioned, laughing.

Sarah also laughed. "Yeah, that probably has something to do with it." She tried to change the subject. "So, how was the bonfire last week?" She was so busy taking care of her dad all week that she had missed school. As she was listening to Stina talk, she noticed something out of the corner of her eye.

Stina rambled on. "Well, Wyatt and Jessica are finally going out. Can you believe it?" Stina continued to elaborate on Wyatt and Jessica and how they finally held hands at the bonfire and so it was just plain obvious that they were together. Her words began to blend together, echoing insignificantly in Sarah's mind.

There was something strange in the corner of the living room. It was a picture, or a painting, and it was casually leaning against the wall. She had never seen it before. It was a painting of a house. She picked it up. It was heavy, and it had a fake gold frame around it. She focused on the picture, the phone being held up to her ear by her shoulder while Stina continued with her story. First, why would there be a painting in her house? Her dad couldn't stand paintings in the house, and she was pretty sure that it wasn't there before she went on her run. Second, the house in the painting wasn't just any house; it was their house. Their little green two-storied house. The forest was painted beautifully behind it. The trees were a deep green and, to her astonishment, there was something else present in the painting. There was color winding around the trees. It was moving subtly, or so it seemed to be. Sarah thought about the painting she saw all those years ago in her grandfather's secret meeting. Could this be that same painting?

The memory of sneaking into that meeting came trampling in; the painting on her grandfather's desk back then whirled around in the same way. Sarah gasped. She dropped the phone and brought the painting right up to her face. It smelled of pine trees and metal. Were her eyes tricking her? They had before. But she couldn't deny it, it was right there, the same shimmering substance that she could see in the forest. She reached out to touch the painting, but she couldn't feel any surface, her finger went through. The painting slipped out of her hands to the floor.

"Hello? … Hello?" Sarah heard Stina's voice coming from the phone.

Sarah promptly picked it up, kicking the weird painting away from her. She must have really been seeing things now. She could have sworn her finger went through the painting.

"What is this?" she whispered.

"Sarah?" Stina shouted from the phone.

"Hi, sorry, I just found the weirdest thing." She lifted the living room blinds so she could watch out for her dad's car driving in.

"Well, what is it? Did you hear anything that I just told you?" Stina asked.

"Um, yeah." She tried to remember the conversation. "Yeah, finally, Jessica and Wyatt! Was Lucas there? The new student?" Lucas was an international student from Brazil who most of the girls had a crush on. Sarah tried to keep the conversation light, but she couldn't stop staring at the painting.

"Oh, of course, and he sat by me, the entire night," Stina boasted. "Aren't you also wondering if James was there?"

"I was trying not to bring it up," Sarah sighed; she noticed the painting whirling around faster.

Stina continued, "Well, he asked about you."

This just frustrated Sarah even more. She felt like she was missing out on so much. She noticed another caller trying to reach her. "I better go. I'll see you tomorrow at school."

"K, well, let me know if your night gets any weirder," Stina said.

She switched to the other line. "Hello?"

The voice was deep and unsettling. "Is this Sarah Carlson?"

"Yes, it is," Sarah said.

"This is the police, and we have a man who claims to be your father here in custody. Stanley Carlson?" the man asked.

"Yes, yes that's him." Sarah sat down carefully as her heart started to feel like it was beating out of her chest. "What? What happened?!"

She tried to remain calm and to steady her shaking hand that was holding the phone.

"Your father is under arrest for attempted armed robbery and, well, it's best for you to come in and hear the rest. Please stay calm and someone will be sent out for you shortly."

"What do you mean arrested? My dad has episodes, he might not have taken his medication. He ..." Tears welled up and she couldn't finish or explain it any further. How could she explain her dad's issues over the phone? She couldn't. They wouldn't get it.

She looked up the number to her grandfather's seniors' home. It was 9:30 p.m. and he was probably in bed, but she thought it would be good for him to know. She picked up the landline phone and called. The front desk responded, saying that he had turned in for the night and was probably sleeping.

"It's an emergency. Tell him his son is in trouble, and I need his help," Sarah pleaded.

"Are you okay, dear?" The lady at the desk sounded very concerned.

"I just really need to speak to my grandfather, please," Sarah begged.

"I'll go wake him, please hold." The lady's voice was sympathetic.

Sarah had never felt so alone or helpless. Who was she to turn to but her grandfather? But he lived in the seniors' home. He required extra care which limited him from coming and going as he wished.

The secretary was back on the line. "Sarah, we checked on your grandfather and he doesn't seem to be in his room. He could be on a walk about the residence, so we will go and look for him." She paused. Another voice spoke in the background. "Well, actually, it looks like he signed out earlier today. He said he was going to his son's place."

"Well, I didn't see him here at all," Sarah said. It was strange for her grandfather to not be in his room at night. He always preferred to settle in early.

"Did he have anywhere else he needed to go?"

"I don't know. I don't know." Sarah's voice faltered.

"We will be in touch with you when we find his whereabouts," the voice said.

Her grandfather wasn't where he was supposed to be, her father was in custody.

She decided to text Stina.

Sarah: Something happened and my dad's in trouble.

Stina: What?! Are you ok?

Sarah: They told me that they are coming to get me and will bring me to the police station. My dad's been arrested.

Her cell phone began to ring. It was Stina. "Why has your dad been arrested? Why don't you come stay with us tonight? I can see if my mom can drive over to pick you up."

"I might take you up on that." She paused, hearing someone knocking on the door. "OK, the police are here. I better go."

Sarah opened the door. A female police officer was standing there, and she could see the police car with another officer inside.

"Hello, Sarah Carlson?" she asked while looking over Sarah's shoulders, as if she'd seen someone else in the house.

Sarah nodded.

The police officer continued, "I know this is a lot of information for you, but your father is in custody in the local jail and you're going to need to come with us, since your father is still your legal guardian."

Sarah looked back at the strange painting. Maybe her grandfather was right, she should just ignore the strange things that she saw. Just forget all about it. No one would understand anyway. But deep down, she felt like there had to be a reason for what she saw, there had to be something more. She pushed those thoughts away. Now wasn't the time for reflection. She left the painting behind and told herself she would look at it again once she returned to her house. Sarah stepped into the police vehicle and looked back at her home. Just as they drove off, she saw something move in the living room window.

"Wait. Stop! There's someone in my house! I saw someone in the window!" Sarah shouted. Her heart was pounding. The thought that someone was in there without her knowing freaked her right out.

The police driver slowly pulled over. "Are you sure?"

"Yes, there's someone walking in the living room. Someone tall! It's not my grandfather, that's for sure."

The police officer in the passenger seat got out of the car and walked up to the house, with the driver following. Sarah got out behind them. The second officer carefully walked into the home and looked around, and after a couple of minutes, he came back out. "There's no one there, Sarah." He stood in the doorway.

Sarah walked up the steps and investigated the house herself. She immediately turned towards the living room where the strange painting was, but it wasn't there. The person that she saw must have taken it.

"But I saw someone in the window. And the … the painting is gone. There was a painting in our living room and it's not there now." Sarah looked around the living room one last time. The police officers looked at each other before proceeding out the door. "The person wouldn't have gotten far. Shouldn't you look for him?"

"Sarah, this isn't just a way to delay us from doing our jobs is it?" The police officer looked annoyed.

"No sir, I'm sorry. I mean, I saw someone, I swear." Her voice faltered. Explaining the painting wouldn't make sense to anyone. Even if she had seen someone in the house, would it matter? Her father was in jail now, and who knew where she would be going? She followed the police out the door, looking back one last time into the empty house. The back door was locked. Everything confused her. Why was she seeing things? And now she was seeing people? She knew deep down that she had seen someone in there. She knew it.

They were all silent as they entered the vehicle for the second time. The ride was long; the darkness of the roads seemed alive, like it would swallow them up. The police officers were talking between themselves.

At the police station, she saw her dad, head hanging down, behind the bars of a temporary cell.

"Dad!" Her emotions surprised her, the loneliness she felt seemed to lurch out of her, deeply in pursuit of someone who knew her, who cared.

"Sarah!" His voice sounded tired, his eyes were bloodshot, his shirt bloodied. Sarah's heart started to pound.

She was looking at the patch of blood on the side of his head. Her voice quaked. "What happened to you, Dad?!"

The police officer came up to her to try and calm her down. "It's okay. Please, just take a deep breath and come with me."

Sarah felt like screaming, "Leave me alone!" She looked around, shook off the officer's hand. "I need to talk to him. What happened, Dad?!" The tears were desperate; she wanted answers.

"It's OK, officer. Please, let me speak to her quickly," Stanley said.

"Five minutes," the officer said, and stepped back.

"It's my head." He breathed in deeply and looked over at another fellow who was in the cell with him. The man had grim eyes, a thick mustache, balding head, and he was watching Stanley's every move while chewing on a toothpick. "I was experiencing another vision. When you left for your run, I kept seeing her, this woman. This woman." He paused and shook his head. "It was like I was supposed to know her, but I don't. But what if, what if it's a long-lost memory that I have, from before. Before the accident."

Sarah was confused by his reasoning but tried to listen and understand, tears streaming down her face. "Before the accident? That doesn't make any sense, Dad. Why does any of this matter?" Sarah urgently shot out her words. "How does this have anything to do with you being in jail? We have to focus on getting you out of here!"

Her dad continued. "I'm just questioning what I know and what … what they all tell me. But lately, I have been seeing things and remembering stuff. This woman, she was calling out to me, from some place that was foreign. She reached out. As if she needed help. But I couldn't save her. And there's more. She was wearing a necklace. This special necklace. Didn't you say something about grandfather receiving a necklace? In the memory you recently had?"

His eyes looked out past Sarah and straight at the wall behind her. His words were jumbled but he was eager to share his revelation. "I keep seeing the necklace and the pawnshop, Holden's Pawnshop, you know the place. I saw a strange man put it there. Believe me, Sarah, I was taking my medication. Well, except for today and yesterday." He said the last part under his breath.

"Dad, why do you keep doing this? Why do you keep trying the 'no medication' thing? It hasn't got you where you think it will." Sarah's words felt pointless, like they held no power. *He's heard it all before, he knows what helps and what doesn't.*

"I …" He looked around. "I don't need it, I don't want it anymore."

"I know. I know you don't want to take it, Dad." Sarah tried to understand. "But, listen to yourself, you're talking about a woman and a necklace? It doesn't make sense. And that memory I had … it is meaningless. The necklace is meaningless."

The police were looking antsy, ready to step in again, concerned for Sarah and ready to move ahead.

"Listen to me, I didn't hurt the clerk. I don't even

remember seeing him there. The place was supposed to be closed." He was trying to get his words in fast.

"Dad—what did you do?" Sarah's voice shook, her hand gripped a bar of the cell.

"Nothing." He looked down, searching for words. "Well, I tried the door to see if it was open, even though the shop was closed, and it was. So, I stepped in and called out to see if anyone was there. I needed to see if the necklace was there. I needed something concrete to prove that my vision held meaning and a connection to reality." He moved closer to the bars; spit flew out of his mouth. "You have to find it, Sarah. The woman was wearing it. I can't be sure who brought it to the pawnshop, but it might have been this woman. But then … your grandfather was wearing it too. In the picture. I can't remember exactly. Maybe there's more than one."

He put his hands on his head and pressed it, as if to give himself relief from the headache.

Sarah's words escaped her, they left her with nothing. It was all too much to take in and she had nothing else to put out. She shook her head in disbelief; her dad wasn't making sense. It was all so illogical. She had never heard him talk about the necklace before. Why was it so important? Was he really remembering things? Or was he confusing her memory with his? Sarah's mind flooded with questions. She thought about her own recent vision and the experience in the forest. Her hand felt over the pocket of her hoodie. The strange key that she'd found was still there. Tears filled her eyes. It all meant nothing. They had to ignore it, they had to.

Her dad continued, seeing that the police were coming back to take Sarah away. "I didn't do anything." He then stood up and reached through the cell bars to grab her hand. "I didn't do anything, trust me on that. I didn't hurt that man. Someone else did. There's something strange about that pawnshop. They are hiding something." He was gripping her hands hard and, in his hands, he had something that was folded up and he gave it to her. "The necklace is in this picture. A week ago, I found these pictures and this one caught my eye, I couldn't look away. Then I thought about your memory about grandfather receiving the necklace. That's why I stopped taking my medication. Whenever I go off the medication, for whatever reason, I feel like my memory is coming back. My memory from ten years ago, Sarah. From before the accident. It's painful because of the migraines, the blackouts. But it's worth it, Sarah." Sarah could see that he was almost smiling. "And this necklace. You've got to go get it, Sarah."

Sarah couldn't help but feel angry. Her dad was in this mess of a predicament all because of some stupid necklace. "Dad, you aren't making sense. How could a necklace be that important? You're more important. And now look at you, you're behind bars because of it? Please, Dad, there's gotta be more," Sarah said. She turned to see the police officer coming to retrieve her.

"Time's up," the officer said, looking at the father, now kneeling at the prison bars in front of his daughter.

"There is more. Trust me, Sarah. I … I don't know what these hallucinations are all about. But I will find out." His voice fell into an exhausted whisper.

She stared at her father in his helpless state, tears welling up in her eyes. She thought about mentioning that she had seen someone in the house, along with the strange painting, but then decided against it.

"Come with me please." The officer motioned for Sarah to follow her into another room.

Stanley continued to plead. "Someone else was there, in the pawnshop, when I got there, so then I freaked out and left immediately, but … but …" He was stumbling around, trying to choose the right words. "The police showed up before I could get away." He stood up and watched as Sarah was led away. "Don't believe what they say! I was set up, Sarah."

"It's OK, Dad, we will get you out of here." Her tears choked her voice.

"Trust me, Sar," his voice shouted after her. "There's more. There's more."

They led her out the door and as she walked out, she unfolded the paper that he had given her. Crinkled as it was, she could see that it was the same photo of Grandpa, Sarah, and Dad going fishing. Her dad was right, there was something sparkling under her grandfather's shirt, that was partially unbuttoned in the hot sun. It was a necklace. A silver chain with an oval pendant on it, crimson in color. Although she had seen the picture before, she had never noticed the necklace. Her mind then went to the memory of her grandfather in his office during his secret meeting. He was wearing the same necklace he had been given that day; it had the image of the keys on it. Keys. No wonder her grandfather was surprised when he looked at the drawing she had made of the keys. She gripped the photo in her fist then folded it up and placed it in her pocket as they entered the main office at the police station.

CHAPTER 4

It had been a week since the incident. The law required that a child with no legal guardian had to be put into foster care until the child turned eighteen, still under the care of the government. Sarah read the pamphlets that the social worker provided before shoving them into the backpack that Stina had lent her. Thankfully, Stina had lent her everything she needed for the past week. Now that the social worker was selected and available, she was able to have the governmental supervision necessary to go back to her house to collect her other things. She glanced into the bag again; the key that she'd found in the forest twinkled from within. Her head throbbed as she flashed back to the moment when she found the key, right before she discovered that her father was missing. She exhaled, and zipped up the bag, as if to stop any opportunity to overanalyze the situation.

"I promise you, my dad has always been good to me and I am responsible enough to take care of myself," Sarah insisted. They were sitting in yellow leather chairs in a brightly lit room covered in floral wallpaper. A chipper lady was working at the desk and answering phone calls.

Karen, the social worker, was bustling about getting papers ready and organizing information for Sarah. Her hair was dark and curly, and she had it pulled back into a rose-colored clip. She finally took a seat on one of the chairs beside Sarah. She had her purse and files placed on her lap.

"Yes, and that may be true." She stood up, placing her items on the couch beside her. "But the law is the law."

After being granted permission to stay at her friend's family's home for the week, she was able to drive to her own home with the social worker to pack up more of her things. She considered that maybe this time away would allow her to paint more. Sarah felt bad thinking that, because it meant that she wouldn't be near her dad and she hated that thought. She was to move into her prescribed foster home for the remainder of the school year, or at least up until her eighteenth birthday, which was in December. She would be required to finish the school year, but could move out on her own then if she wanted. "There are many others who have been in your situation, Sarah. They too say they are responsible." She gave a warm smile. Sarah tried to smile back. "The reality is that the law is the law, so we must move forward and have the best attitudes that we can, right?"

Karen drove Sarah back to her neighborhood. Sarah felt anxious as she entered the house. The last time she had stepped into her home it was to look for the man that she thought she saw, and the painting. She entered the living room first and looked around again, hoping the painting would be there, but it was still missing.

"What are you looking for?" Karen asked.

"There was just this strange …" She stood back up after peering under the couch and looked at Karen. She had learned not to share with others about her strange sightings;

there wasn't any point. "Oh, it's nothing really. So, when can I see my dad next?" Sarah changed the subject.

Karen began to look around. "You can see him later today, once things are finalized."

"What things?" Sarah felt like she was in the dark. Everyone else knew what was going on, except for her. "And if you don't mind, why are you looking around my house?"

She stopped and moved back toward Sarah. "I'm sorry, dear, but you are going to have to let me do my job, and right now, it's to inspect where you used to live. It's to give your new guardians an idea of what they will be dealing with when they take you in."

Karen continued, "Your father suggested an aunt of his, she would be your great aunt of course. She goes by the name Gale. Do you remember your Aunt Gale?"

Sarah was confused. "No, I don't." She looked down, anger rising. "At all."

Karen, unfazed by Sarah's attitude, continued, "Well, your father does, and that's good that he thought of her, because since she is family, if she agrees to take you in, then you can live with her, and not a foster family."

Sarah was semi-relieved. She was certain she had no family other than her dad and grandfather, no aunts or uncles that she knew of.

"When I spoke to your father, he said that your grandfather informed him that you used to go to Gale's for dinners quite often," Karen said. "It's good for him to have these warm memories to think about, since I'm sure he struggles with remembering anything past ten years ago. You would have been at these family meals too, you know."

Sarah didn't remember. She didn't remember being introduced to an Aunt Gale at all. At family meals, she only remembered her dad and grandfather. Grandfather always had to fill Sarah and her father in on memories that they would have had, they *should* have had, and it was getting old.

She just wished that she and her father could have real, genuine memories of their own. She sat on the couch, ignoring the fact that Karen was still snooping through the house. She continued to scour the living room with her eyes, hoping she would find a trace of the strange painting, even though she already knew it was gone when she had come in with the police officers. Her mind went back to when she first saw it. She had picked it up, and when she touched it, her hand went through it. It was like the painting in her vision. She thought about the man she had seen in the house when she drove off with the police. Why was he in the house, and why did he take the painting? He must have put it there in the first place. Maybe he had something to do with her dad being in jail.

There is more, there is more. The words from her dad echoed in her mind. Maybe there was more to their entire story. How could they know that they were receiving accurate information about their past? She shook off the thoughts.

"Sarah?" Karen looked at Sarah. Her voice seemed to echo. "Are you OK? Is it the migraines?"

"I'm fine. How do you know about my migraines?" Sarah asked.

"It looked like you had a bit of a headache, that's all," Karen quickly responded. Sarah found it strange that Karen knew about her migraines. Maybe her dad had time to fill her in? She didn't know.

"I was just thinking. So many strange things have been happening, but it's not worth talking about. Really." Sarah paused. "There was a random painting here before I went to the police station last week and it just seemed to disappear. I just don't know where it would be," she shared, even though she knew that Karen wouldn't really be able to help. "The thing is, I don't know how it even got into the house. I thought I saw someone else in here that night, too. But that was a week ago now."

Karen looked surprised. She paused in place. "I sure don't see a painting in here. I thought your dad didn't like any sort of art in the house."

"How do you know that?" Sarah asked. It confused her that she would know about her life in that much detail.

Karen was stifled. "Oh, well, I can just tell. There's nothing on the walls but shelves."

She was right, Sarah thought. Maybe it was that obvious.

"Is there any chance that I could live with my friend's family, since I'm closer to them?" Sarah asked.

Karen briefly looked through the shoebox of pictures before placing them on the footstool next to her dad's chair. "Honey, believe me, it would be nice if you could go wherever you want to, but the law is the law. Family is always the next guardian of choice."

Sarah thought about how Karen must deal with orphans and foster children all the time. She was just another number to add to her "files."

Sarah smiled sadly. "If only my grandfather could take me, it would be my first choice." She paused, thinking about her next words. She then turned abruptly towards Karen. "That's why I need to do all that I can to make sure my dad is released."

Karen remained calm. "Well, yes. I applaud you for your enthusiasm. You will be busy finishing up your school year, and you can leave justice to the police, OK?"

Her "OK" really upset Sarah. Was there really nothing she could do? She was the powerless one.

"They will do the best they can. Your dad wants you to finish the school year well."

Sarah looked up, tears pricking the back of her eyes. How could Karen know everything her dad wanted? "You have no idea what he wants, neither do the police, or Gale! I will do whatever I need to do to make sure that he is free."

Both of them looked at each other. Karen looked lost as to what she would respond with. Instead, she smiled sympathetically, and picked up a tissue box and passed it to her.

"Guess what, Sarah."

Sarah dabbed her eyes and waited for what Karen was going to say.

"Soon you'll be able to do what you want. But right now, let the professionals help you out." Karen laughed. "Believe me, we could all use a little professional help." She then regained a serious tone. "There are bigger things at play, some things that you may not understand just yet."

"What bigger things?" Sarah said.

Karen didn't respond. Maybe it wouldn't be so bad, Sarah thought. But if her father were convicted, it meant jail for up to nine years. Even if she could be free to do what she wanted, she felt she couldn't leave this town.

Sarah went upstairs to pack a bag with clothes, toiletries, and some personal items like her journal. But her journal was nowhere to be found. She looked in all the usual places, but it wasn't anywhere. There had been people in the house since her dad got arrested. People like police officers, and possibly Grandfather, and that other person that she saw. That only *she* saw. The shadow in the window that belonged with that painting. He was in here. But why would he want her journal? It had to be in the room. She double-checked the places where she usually put it, but still, she couldn't find anything. She suddenly felt scared to be in her own home. Karen waited in her bedroom doorway.

"I wanna get out of here," Sarah said.

"What are you looking for?" Karen asked.

She took a deep breath. "My journal. I have a ton of drawings and personal stuff in it." Sarah looked around the room.

"Oh, it will probably turn up, Sarah. For now, don't worry about it. We need to get going if you're going to make it in time to see your dad at visiting hour."

"Right." Seeing her dad was more important. She picked up the duffel bag that was filled with clothes before following Karen down the stairs.

SARAH WAS IN THE VISITOR'S ROOM AT THE PRISON. THERE WAS a clear windowpane between them and microphones to speak into; security guards stood behind her and behind her father. The room had a smell of dust and metal.

"Your eyes are less bloodshot, Dad. You're making sure that they give you your medication?" Sarah wanted to be able to hug her dad, to get him out of the prison. "This isn't fair. Why can't we speed up the trial so that the truth can be revealed and you can be free?"

"There is nothing that we can do other than hope, Sarah, and if you …" He paused, unsure if he should continue. "Grandfather came in with his nurses the other day. It was good to see him, but I don't know how many more visits he will be making. His condition worsens. I am so sorry. I wish there was someone there for you."

Sarah looked down, trying to save the big tears for when she was away from her dad; she didn't want to make it harder on him.

"The thing is, I think we found someone. Grandfather and I were talking about my Aunt Gale. Grandfather's younger sister. She's in great health, in her seventies. She lives in a very nice home with tons of room available. Sounds like she is willing to take you in while you finish your final year of school."

"Yes, Karen told me," Sarah said, looking down.

"Well, what do you think?" he asked.

"I think that I wish I could stay in my own home, my own room, and that Grandfather could move in with me and that you could be out of jail," Sarah blurted out.

"Yes, we all wish that." Stanley exhaled.

"What's going to happen to the house?" Sarah asked.

"Well, the neighbors are going to watch it and Grandfather is going to make sure it's rented out to a nice family," Stanley answered, looking around briefly.

Sarah nodded silently. "OK, well, this aunt's house sounds fine, and it's only until December." She wanted to vocalize the fact that she turned eighteen in December and therefore could make her own decisions after that. "I'll do what I have to do. When I turn eighteen, I'm going to move out on my own."

"Okay, you have my permission." Her dad smiled, relieved that his daughter was cooperating. "Of course, you'll need enough money for rent and all of that."

"At least I'll be able to graduate with my friends, maybe stay with them from time to time. And of course, visit you every day," Sarah continued. She gave a weak smile.

Her dad didn't respond; he just looked down, back at the security guards, and then back at Sarah.

"What, Dad?" Sarah said. "There's more, isn't there?"

The signal went off; the speaking sessions were done.

"Sarah, it's for the best, trust me on this. You want more family, right?"

She knew he was going to add details that she wouldn't like. She replied, "I don't care what I said before about wanting more family. I … I am happy with just you and

Grandfather, honestly!" She exhaled and looked at her dad. "What are you saying?"

"Aunt Gale lives in another town," he said.

Sarah shot up. "What?!"

"It's a town called Walton. It's a bit up north."

"North? How far up north?"

"It's in Canada." He quickly followed the news with detail, as if to alleviate any stress. "It's by the ocean, it's beautiful, there are tons of forests with trails." He tried to say all the good stuff, knowing that it would not magically make it all better.

"What about school?! Why can't I finish school with my friends?" she asked.

"It was either Aunt Gale or a foster home that already has three other"— he cleared his throat—"troubled youths. And these kids have been through a lot. I didn't want to subject you to that type of dynamic. With everything that has been going on in your life, this is a chance for you to start fresh. You can still see your friends on weekends. There's a train that goes directly to Walton, about eight hours' journey north." He shuffled on his seat. "People around here, they know what happened to me. I don't want you to live with the weight of it all, with people asking you questions about the case all the time. In Walton, you can be a new you!"

Sarah could tell he struggled with that last sentence.

"I …" Her voice felt weak. She was tired of arguing. "I really don't want to be a new me, I don't want to do anything different. I just want you out of here. I need to make sure you are out of here." The big tears were starting now, she couldn't wait.

"Time to go," a voice bellowed from a tired-looking security guard. He looked at Sarah and then motioned for her father to get moving. "Say your goodbyes."

"Sarah. I love you. Trust me on this." His eyes were welling up too.

Sarah shook as she cried. "Every single time, I get pulled around, taking care of you and your hallucinations, your amnesia. Missing out on stuff. And now, you send me even further away from you? I'm the only family YOU have!"

Her dad had to go. Sarah was left on the other side of the glass, with the emptiness and anger of not being able to say "I love you" back, or talk things through. The echo of the prison door slamming as her dad left the room was like a gong in her mind.

Karen waited for her behind the door. As Sarah walked out, she held out a hot chocolate that she had picked up for her, but Sarah didn't take it. She couldn't face having to explain any of her feelings to anyone. All she wanted was a few minutes more with her dad.

WITH ALL HER BOXES AND BAGS IN THE TRUNK OF KAREN'S car, they took off for the train station, and the train that would take her to the place called Walton. Her heart sank at the thought that her journal was still missing. She felt like she had no say about anything, and she hated it. "So that's it, I have no choice but to go to this Gale's house?" Sarah gave it one last go.

"Right now, it's the way it looks like it's going to go. Your father and grandfather both want this for you. It's eight hours away and you can come back on weekends occasionally, stay with your friends, visit with your dad. It will be OK," Karen said, while they got settled into the vehicle. Sarah couldn't believe what was happening, and all so fast. She had already missed two weeks of school and so many running practices. She messaged her best friends, Stina and Tracey, telling them what the plan was. Karen pulled into the parking lot at the train station. There were twenty minutes until departure. "You get out here and I'll go purchase your ticket."

Just as Sarah jumped out of the car, Tracey pulled up in her vehicle and Stina's dad pulled in beside Tracey with Stina waving out the window. Sarah found it hard to say goodbye, but she was thankful for her friends. She knew she would always have a support network here. She was determined to get back to Augusta as soon as she could.

"I guess I should give you your bag back," Sarah said to Stina.

"Nah, keep it. You can use it as your travel bag when you come visit on the weekends," Stina reassured her.

"You always have a place to stay with us," Stina's dad said. "We'd love to have you at our place for as long as you want, when it's possible."

"Thanks so much. I wish it didn't have to be this way," Sarah replied.

They gave each other hugs and said their goodbyes. Sarah turned towards Karen who was walking briskly, ticket in hand.

"Be sure to call once you arrive." Karen said quickly. "Now go on."

She took the ticket, thanked Karen, and before she knew it, she was on the train, headed for the town of Walton, by the sea.

CHAPTER 5

*S*he awoke as the train came to a halt. Sarah looked out the window to see a train station much like the one she had left behind. Walking off the train, she headed over to retrieve her luggage and out of the corner of her eye, she saw a woman in her seventies, dressed in navy blue dress pants and a floral blouse. Her hair was white and grey, and in a loose bun. She was hanging onto a leather purse.

"Sarah?" She waved.

That must be her, thought Sarah, as she grabbed some of her bags. The woman walked toward her.

Sarah reluctantly smiled. "Gale?"

Gale smiled and laughed. "Hello, Sarah! Call me Auntie Gale! No need to put the *great* in front of it, I am as young as I feel. Don't feel a day past thirty!" She struggled to pick up one of Sarah's bags. "Maybe make that sixty."

Sarah felt a slight laugh escape her.

"Why don't I drive the van around?" Gale suggested. "You seem to have a lot of luggage here."

Sarah agreed, and she dragged her bags as close to the

road as she could. Gale seemed nice, but she couldn't help but feel homesick. Homesick for her home and for her dad and grandfather. But it wasn't just that. She also felt homesick for something that she couldn't even describe. It was as if she was missing something, or like she had forgotten something, but was grasping at straws to distinguish what it was. All her muddled memories and the blurred years before the accident sloshed around in her mind. The strange idea that she was missing something, forgetting something, was always in her thoughts. Sarah saw Gale approaching. Her glasses were on the edge of her nose, almost ready to fall off.

"Let's get you home and settled in, then we can have some tea and talk about school," Gale said, trying to be extra positive.

Heaviness crept in over Sarah; she was not looking forward to starting fresh in a new school, where friendships were already established, and groups settled. She had no desire to try and fit in. All she wanted to do was to fall asleep and wake up on the weekend when she could go stay at Stina's and catch up on all the happenings of her old life.

She slid the van's side door open and started loading her bags. Gale helped. Sarah then jumped into the back seat.

"Oh, you don't want to sit up front?" Gale said.

"Oh, OK, sure." She obliged and climbed into the front passenger seat.

They drove through the town. It was small and quaint, with little shops lining the streets, what she assumed to be downtown. And then there it was, the ocean. The salty air rushed through their rolled down windows. The familiarity of the ocean scent calmed her somehow.

"Amazing isn't it. The ocean." Gale tried to make conversation.

"Yes, it's similar in Augusta, definitely more remote here."

She strived to hold up her end of the conversation. Augusta really wasn't that similar. The Kennebec River wasn't the ocean, but there was something about the water that did make her feel at home.

Gale looked over to her, then back to the road. "We live up on that hill. It's beautiful because we can see the ocean from our kitchen window, and the forest, with running trails, is in our backyard."

Sarah tried not to look impressed.

"Your grandfather says you like to run."

"Yeah, it's OK." She didn't want to talk anymore. Of course she loved running, of course. "So, you're my grandpa's sister?"

"Yes, his younger, spry sister!" Gale replied.

They pulled up to a picturesque garden house. There were some other homes nestled in the woods nearby. The woods behind the house looked very rich and full of life. Sarah felt a subtle hint of excitement, but then she considered her friends back at home and realized that they would be heading to running practice soon. Her heart sank.

"Your room is up the stairs, the first room on the right. Make yourself at home. I'll be in the garden. Dinner will be at five."

Gale didn't help her with her bags. Sarah lugged them up the stairs and turned into the bedroom. It was a large room, plain, with one set of drawers beside the bed. The window overlooked the backyard and garden.

Dinner was served around a circular wooden table with a red tablecloth. Old fashioned dishes were used, with flower designs around the edges, and the food was delicious. Gale had made chicken pot pie, and it was steaming hot and filled with vegetables and meat. Sarah looked around the room while she ate. There was nothing on the walls, no decorations. Everything was simple and minimalistic. Empty.

"The school is not far from here, about a ten-minute walk —that is, at the pace you go. For people like me, it's more like half an hour," Gale explained. "Your teachers know that you will be starting tomorrow, and they know a little about your story."

Sarah didn't like the sound of that. "How much do they know?"

"They know enough to make your transition comfortable." Gale offered Sarah some juice. "We talked to the principal the other day. We shared some of your story, that your dad is in jail and that you don't have a mother. We didn't explain the full details of your father's case."

"I have a mother. Had a mother," Sarah objected. She moved her glass closer to the pour. Gale did not respond to her comment.

"Thank you." She tried to be polite as she received the juice. She needed to give this aunt of hers a chance. Or at least, she should try to.

The evening grew dim. She said goodnight to Gale and climbed up the stairs. Sitting on her bed, she looked at her phone and considered texting her dad, only to remember that he didn't have his phone in jail. She missed him, missed the security of having a dad nearby who loved her, in his own way. Loneliness crept in. She felt strange being in a different house, a house that was so empty, and with a relative that she didn't even know about until now. She closed the blinds and thought about unpacking, but group-texted her friends instead.

Stina: How's the first day there? Is your aunt cool?

Sarah: She is fine, nice enough, I guess.

Stina: You hardly know her, it seems weird that your dad agreed to send you there.

Tracey: Well, she is a relative. He thought it was nice that you would get a chance to get to know her.

Sarah: Say hi to coach and everyone for me. I start school tomorrow, I'll let you know how it goes.

Stina: Tomorrow is the big race, you really should be in it.

Not only was her father in jail, but she was missing out on everything, all the good parts of her life, the things that she enjoyed. She now had to leave it all behind. How could this happen? Why did she have to be sent away? Emotion stirred in her heart. She wanted to run out of the house, and run all her problems away. If only her dad hadn't gone to the stupid pawnshop, she thought to herself. If only he'd taken his medication, and listened to Grandpa, then none of this would have happened. Her face felt warm, tears arrived, and she felt like crying hard. She missed her dad so much, but knew that she had to be brave.

Swallowing back the tears, she walked toward the window and looked outside. Her hands gripped the windowsill as if it was the only thing that she could confide in. Her eyes searched the sky, and then she closed them, exhaling. There was nothing she could do, she felt stuck in the situation. She had to ride it out, ride out the year of school. For her dad. She would do this for her dad. She sat down on the bed. Her mind immediately started going over the night that her dad got arrested and how it all happened while she was on her half-hour run. Why was the necklace so important to him? She brainstormed all the possibilities as she stared at the crinkled picture that her father had given her. Her eyes focused on the necklace. It was the same one that was in the memory that came to her from her grandfather's office. Next time she was back in Maine, she knew that she had to try and find it.

She stared up at the ceiling but as her eyes moved past the bag that Stina had given her, she noticed it was glowing from within. She walked over to the bag and unzipped it slowly. The strange key that she had found was still there. She had almost forgotten about it altogether, but now it was illuminated somehow. She stepped back and her headache began. Sarah reached in and picked up the key. It was warm. She spun it around and inspected it. She brought the strange key back to her bed. Sarah's eyes were heavy. Key still in hand, she breathed in deeply and fell asleep.

Sunlight streamed through the slight opening in the curtains of Sarah's bedroom. It was time to get up and venture into this new school. Sarah noticed that she was still holding onto the strange key. She put it in her sweater pocket and zipped it up before wandering into the kitchen. Gale was there with some oatmeal on the stove.

"Would you like some? There is also some cereal on the counter," she pointed out.

"Thanks." Sarah took a bowl that was on the counter and Gale scooped some oatmeal into it.

"How was your sleep?" Gale inquired.

"It was good, thanks. Yours?" Sarah asked. Gale took some milk out of the fridge and Sarah noticed how empty it was. There was only a small amount of food in it. If Gale lives on her own, that would make sense, she reasoned to herself.

"Wonderful, as usual." Gale said.

Sarah quickly ate and then got her backpack ready. "I think I'll just walk to school."

"I can drive you today and then you can try the trails

tomorrow, how about that?" Gale suggested. "Might be nice to have a ride for your first day."

Sarah agreed. Gale had the car running when she went outside.

They drove for a couple of minutes without talking.

"I know this must be quite a change for you." Gale finally spoke. "Having to move for your last year of school."

"Yeah, it is," Sarah acknowledged. Her eyes gazed upon the fall leaves starting to appear on the trees that lined the dirt road into the small town of Walton. "I wish I was back home with my dad." She looked at Gale, hoping she hadn't hurt her feelings.

"Of course! These things are never easy," Gale said. "I'm glad your grandfather arranged for me to help out."

"Yeah. I wonder why we didn't meet until now?" Sarah asked.

"Well, you would have been over when you were really young, before the …" She stopped and looked at Sarah.

"It's OK. You're meaning before the accident," Sarah said.

Gale smiled awkwardly and continued driving. "Thankfully, your grandfather kept in touch and was able to connect us now."

Sarah was left with an empty feeling inside. There always seemed to be so many gaps in her family history, so many questions. Everything was too simple, or just unexplained. Gale drove down the hill and around the corner to where the high school was located. "There it is. You'll just head on in the doors and find Mrs. Sanderson."

"Mrs. Sanderson?" Sarah felt nervous and homesick for her old school.

"She's the principal and she's expecting you," Gale reminded her.

She got out of the car, not waving at Gale as she drove away. Other students immediately started looking at her, not recognizing her, knowing that she was new. She tried to ignore the stares and walked in the front doors. There was a tall woman wearing a black dress and a bright cardigan. She looked like she was a teacher. Sarah decided to approach her. "Excuse me, could you help me find Mrs. Sanderson?"

"She's just in the office, down the hall, to the right," the woman replied. Sarah followed her directions, walking at a faster pace, hoping to avoid people staring at her. She could hear the teacher whispering to another staff member, "Oh, she is the new student."

Sarah rolled her eyes. Everything would have been just fine if she had been able to stay at her home school, and now she was forced into awkwardness. She was stuck with a stranger who was supposed to be family, but her dad couldn't be there to make the interactions easier. Her father couldn't even check on her. She heard a text come through.

Stina: Have a good first day at school-miss ya!

She put her phone back in her pocket and continued to walk down the hall. There was a group of girls leaning against the lockers, talking about something seemingly very important. One of them eyed Sarah as she walked by, unimpressed. A few guys were joking with one another as they walked beside her, laughing about a goofy thing they had done the night before. *This is exactly like my high school*, she told herself. *It's going to be fine.* She saw where it said "Office" and reached out to open the door but then tripped on something that was in front of her feet, someone's backpack, causing her to fall into the glass door and onto the ground. Chatter and laughing could be heard all around her. A friendly girl walked up to her and asked if she was OK.

"I'm fine, I'm fine," Sarah said, struggling to stand back up.

"Whoa, Leif, watch yourself dude. You completely

destroyed that girl," said a tall, lanky guy wearing a backwards cap.

This "Leif" appeared in front of Sarah, apologetic. "I am so sorry. That would be my backpack in your way." He picked up his backpack. He looked a little nervous himself.

Sarah could feel that she was blushing, and her long hair was in front of her face. She brushed it back and took Leif's hand to stand back up.

"It's fine, thanks." She paused and looked at Leif, but quickly focused back on what she was doing, instead of staring at his face. "Is this the office?"

"Yes, it is." As obvious as it was, the huge sign saying "Office" hanging over the door, Leif was courteous, and he had kind eyes. His lanky friend standing behind him decided he didn't want to wait any longer. Sarah smiled at Leif again and he watched her as she went into the office.

"Hi, I'm supposed to meet with Mrs. Sanderson. Today's my first day. My name is Sarah," she said to the secretary.

"Oh yes, Sarah, welcome. Mrs. Sanderson will be right …" And before she could finish the sentence, Mrs. Sanderson appeared. She had graying hair tied into a bun, and wore bright yellow heels with her black pencil skirt.

"Welcome, I'm Mrs. Sanderson." Sarah shook her hand. "This is your schedule and it looks like you will begin with Mr. Fredericks in Math. Lucky you!" She gave a semi-sarcastic smile. "His class is down the main hall and to the right. You'll see the map on your schedule. Do you have any questions?"

Sarah had tons of questions, but she knew it wasn't the time to ask them all. Mrs. Sanderson then spun around, responding to another teacher who was trying to get her attention.

"Have a great day, Sarah," Mrs. Sanderson quickly added, before immersing herself in conversation with the teacher.

Sarah looked down at her schedule. She walked through the empty halls after receiving further direction from the secretary. Class had already begun and now it was time for her awkward and late entry to Mr. Fredericks' class.

Get this over with, get this over with, she whispered to herself. The school was a lot smaller than the one in Augusta, but it had all the same elements. Dull, cream-colored floors that had a freshly waxed look, lined with identical silver-colored lockers on each side.

Mr. Fredericks' class proved to be as dull as her other math class back home. She got through a couple of other classes and then made it to lunchtime. She finally had some time to find her locker. She put her books in and then found her way outside.

The cool autumn air refreshed her immediately. Everybody had their groups, and rightly so. *They've all known each other for years,* she assumed. It wasn't a large school like hers, but big enough for a grade 9-12 high school. Some kids were playing soccer on the field, the fall trees surrounding it leaving their mark on the ground. Maybe it wouldn't matter if she made friends. This weekend she hoped to take the train back home to attend Tracey's birthday party. She was determined that this was how she would get through this year, weekend visits home, and not worrying about fitting in.

A crowd was gathered by the basketball hoops and some guys were hanging around discussing someone's car. The tall, lanky guy from before was with them. And so was Leif. He seemed so mature and confident compared to other high school guys. She wondered if he would be in any of her afternoon classes. There was a group of girls from her grade, eating lunch on the grass near the guys. She couldn't be bothered trying to talk to anyone. She was texting her friends from home all through lunch anyway. This year will be a breeze, she thought. Her plan was to stay out of everyone's way and be invisible.

Her final class of the day was English. She entered the classroom and immediately her eyes locked on Leif at the back of the class. There were a couple of girls from some of her other classes that she recognized. She sat beside one of them. "Is it OK if I sit here?"

"Yeah, completely," the kind-eyed, brunette girl said.

Meanwhile, Sarah noticed another girl, tall and lean, with a very glamorous outfit on. She was looking annoyed that Sarah had taken that seat and rolled her eyes while finding another seat behind her.

The kind girl saw this too and laughed, "Don't worry, we don't have assigned seats."

"Thanks." Sarah smiled. "I'm Sarah."

"Oh yeah, the new one!" she said. "Everyone's been wondering about you. We've been getting a lot of new students lately it seems. You. And then, Leif. He got here, like, two weeks ago."

Her voice chimed, eager to share info. Sarah looked back at Leif who was sitting a few seats behind them. "Oh, I'm Tindra, by the way."

The other girl who had to switch seats at the last minute leaned into their conversation. "And I'm Christina, the one who usually sits there."

"Christina, seriously?" Tindra reprimanded.

"K, fine, whatever." Christina leaned back in her chair and waited for the teacher to begin.

Sarah tried to stay lighthearted. "Sorry, you can have it back tomorrow."

This comment seemed to amuse Christina. "Not if you get here first though, right?" There was a pause, Sarah uncertain how to respond.

"Don't mind her, she's actually nice sometimes." Tindra eyed Christina.

The teacher came to the center and called for attention. She looked to be in her forties, taller, and had light blond hair braided in the back. "Class, we've got a lot to cover today. But first …" She looked over at Sarah. "I see we have someone new. Another new student. All within a couple days!"

Everyone seemed unimpressed because most of them had met Sarah already in other classes. "My name is Mrs. Lee. And you're Sarah, I presume."

Sarah nodded, hoping the attention would be off her soon. She fiddled with her notebook.

"Welcome, and I am sure that Tindra here can fill you in on any questions you might have about what my expectations are."

Tindra smiled. "Of course!"

"So, today is the first day of our creative writing unit. First, I want everyone to do a free writing exercise. I want you to think back to a time when you were a small child. Think far, far back, the earliest happy memory that you can think of. And the focus is happy memories right now."

Mrs. Lee instructed everyone to take out loose-leaf paper and to start free writing about early memories. She wrote the question on the whiteboard: What is your earliest "happy" memory? The class went quiet and began writing.

The teacher continued, "Our big project for this unit will be on the topic of memories. You will provide a creative writing piece, it can be in the form of a poem, song, or short story, that will go along with a visual representation. You may do a painting, a comic, or short video or series of pictures."

Painting. She would have the opportunity to paint! But she knew she would struggle to think of a happy memory as a child, other than the same one that she always had, that was in her journal. But that memory was more of a vision or dream, it was too abstract. She thought about various ideas, mostly memories of Christmas dinners when she was at the earliest seven or eight, which all occurred after the accident. But memories from when she was smaller than that, she could not retrieve. They were there, somewhat, but they seemed fake, like they were not actually connected to her. The happiest time she could remember, furthest back, genuinely, was when she was eight and she was given a canvas from her teacher to paint on because someone had discovered that she was an excellent artist. She was able to paint on the canvas at recess, and painted freely. This painting was of the blue sky merging into waves from the ocean. It was the first time she had ever painted anything, as far as she could remember. Maybe she had painted before the accident; she didn't know. Her teacher called her a prodigy and a real talent. Her dad, on the other hand, did not acknowledge her skill, even after the continuous encouragement and persuasion from her teacher. That's when the happy memory broke into pieces and Sarah was reminded of her dad's issues.

Tindra, Christina, and the other students were writing quickly, and she decided to get started on the painting idea from grade two.

After about fifteen minutes, the teacher asked for a few people to share.

"Vincent, go ahead." Mrs. Lee called out an intelligent-looking student with glasses and dark hair perfectly brushed back.

"My memory goes back to my fourth birthday party. I was so excited because there was a train birthday cake and I had all my friends over. I felt so big, but I was only four. I remember my whole family and grandparents being over too. My mom cut the cake and laughed when I got it all over my face."

The class seemed to like his memory. They all clapped. Sarah was in awe that he remembered something so far back. Impressive, she thought.

"Okay, Zack, go for it. What is your memory?" The teacher seemed reluctant to call upon this student, and students were quietly laughing even before he spoke.

"Well, my earliest memory goes back all the way to the day I was conceived." The class broke out in laughter and Mrs. Lee rolled her eyes. "It was a night of passion."

Mrs. Lee interrupted, "You know what, Zack, let's keep these G-rated. Think about a different memory and maybe we will come back to you. How about you, Christina?"

Christina waited until the class stopped laughing from Zack's comment, then flipped back her curly black hair, took a breath, and began to share while chewing gum intermittently. "Well, I remember so many things. I feel like I can practically show you an entire movie of my life if I wanted to."

An overweight fellow sitting next to Zack interrupted. "BORING." His laugh was followed by a snort and Zack laughed along with him.

"Okay Jeremy, that is enough. Christina, go ahead," Mrs. Lee calmly encouraged.

"Well, before I was interrupted, I was going to say that I feel like I can remember so many happy things, you know? But I guess if I had to pick one happy memory, the furthest back, it would be when I was a baby, maybe like one year old, and I was in my crib, doing what babies do. I remember my mom and dad singing to me. I remember their faces smiling." Christina stopped, feeling like she had shared all she wanted.

Sarah felt dumbfounded. How could anyone remember

anything from that age, and with so much detail attached to it, including the emotions?

Mrs. Lee was nodding, equally impressed with Christina's story. As if she knew what Sarah was thinking, she commented, "Thank you, Christina. It is quite unique to remember something you experienced as a baby, but it is not impossible. How special for you!"

Sarah sat back. Her heart felt heavy in her chest and she was starting to get a headache. She begged herself not to have a migraine on her first day of school. She had her binder from her old school open to a blank page, and she began to draw instead of continuing to write. Her heart dropped at the thought of her journal being missing. Her pencil outlined the same three keys that she had drawn before, while the students shared their memories.

Mrs. Lee walked by Sarah's desk and looked down. "Did you have anything to share, Sarah? I see you are quite the artist."

Sarah felt a wave of shyness flow over her and she hated it. She usually shared in class, back at her old school.

"Um, sure." She shifted in her seat and began to speak. "My teacher in grade two gave me a canvas to paint on. It was the first time I had ever painted, and I loved it. I was able to paint at recess and created a beautiful picture."

Mrs. Lee waited for a bit before asking, "How old were you when you had that special memory?"

Sarah didn't want to answer but it would be strange if she didn't. "I was eight, I think." Her cheeks felt hot and she hoped the attention would veer away from her.

"You don't have anything else from before that?" Mrs. Lee asked.

Sarah felt her heart beating, she felt so on the spot. "No, no I don't."

"How about from kindergarten or grade one?" she

continued.

"No, I'm sorry, it's just that," Sarah said. She wished she hadn't said that. Now people were going to think she was weird.

She continued doodling, hoping Mrs. Lee would change the subject. Mrs. Lee nodded and then quickly chose someone else to share. Finally, she asked for everyone to hand in what they had written. The students stood up and handed in their work to the teacher, then waited by the door for the bell. Sarah put her binder into her bag and moved toward the door.

"That painting must have been pretty special," a voice said behind her. Startled, Sarah turned around. She blushed when she saw Leif standing behind her.

"Painting?" She forgot for a moment what he was referring to.

"The one in your memory," Leif said. "For the assignment." He smiled and raised his paper up to show Sarah before dropping it off on Mrs. Lee's desk.

"Oh right, that painting." Sarah smiled.

"So, do you still paint?" Leif spoke with a subtle accent.

Sarah suddenly felt nervous. Leif's handsome brown eyes looked into hers with interest. Her thoughts went fuzzy. She stepped back, bumping into a desk. "Not really—" she finally said, looking away from him toward the door.

Just as Leif was about to say something else, the bell rang, and the students began to rush out into the hall, eager to get to their lockers and out the doors.

"See ya, Sarah!" Tindra yelled as she was about to leave. Christina casually waved, too, as she zipped up her designer purse. Sarah waved.

She soon found her way out of the front doors of the school, looking out on the new town that she was now a part of. The school was on a bit of an elevation that allowed her to see the downtown area. There wasn't a lot of traffic on the roads, unlike the roads in Augusta.

Just then, Gale pulled into the school driveway.

Sarah ran up and got into the van. She noticed that Leif was standing near the door, watching her leave. She tried not to look at him, but was annoyed with herself that he made her nervous. She finally looked his way and saw another girl walking up to him. He turned towards her and started talking. Sarah's heart sank a little, but then she swiftly brushed it off. She tried to push away any form of disappointment. She remembered James back in Augusta. Next time she was visiting home she would see him. But none of it mattered. She wouldn't get to go to any of the formals with her friends, let alone James.

Even though it wasn't the school that she was used to, the routine of going to school was the same, just emptier. She breathed deeply. Knowing that she would be back home for the weekend and staying with Stina's family gave her that little spark of hope that she clung to. Karen, the social worker, was OK with it, which was good.

Her heart sank again as she thought about her dad and she hoped that the prison staff would be giving him the medical care that he needed. Her mind bounced directly to how he had been before he had left the house so suddenly, before the incident at the pawnshop. He said he was taking his medication, but that whole week was rough on him for some reason. She recalled how he would be staring off into the distance every so often, and he wouldn't respond when Sarah called his name. Her memories of childhood danced like clouds above her head, something so fleeting, weightless, and fake. She hated to admit it, but it all seemed like a farce. Her whole life. And her dad's hallucinations were the brunt of it because he could never provide the clarity that she was searching for, that she needed.

CHAPTER 7

That evening, Gale was in the room at the back of the kitchen. It looked like a study or an office. Sarah noticed that Gale had disappeared into this room for the majority of the evening, wandering in and out while talking on the phone. She wasn't making much of an effort to get to know Sarah, but in a way, Sarah didn't mind that. Instead, she grabbed her earphones and put a light jacket over her hoodie with the pockets, the key still zipped inside, and went outside for a walk.

It would soon be dusk and there was a quietness in the air that was soothing. Sarah wandered past the trail that Gale said would take her to school, and to her right she noticed another trail that led to a pond and a gazebo. Her eyes looked up into the trees and she could see the familiar shimmer around the branches. She didn't go down any trails, but walked toward the main road that led to the town. She started to see the few houses that lined the streets. People were tucked into their homes, windows illuminated. She could see briefly into one of the houses; it looked like a family was sitting around the table for dinner, she could hear faint laughing. Sarah's heart dipped into nostalgia. She missed family, even if it was just her dad. She veered off the main street towards a hill that overlooked the ocean. The dark blue outline of the water looked painted, like someone just took the brush and dragged it along the horizon. A memory of herself painting at school flashed through her mind.

There was a certain confidence that was attached to her memories of painting, and the idea of painting, but she didn't know why it was there. And she could never understand why her father hated it. Both her grandfather and dad encouraged her to do sports, but never anything that had to do with painting. She thought suddenly of the necklace in the photo. If it was at the pawnshop, how could she get it? How did it relate to her father's situation? There was so much to figure out.

She merged back onto the main street. There was a pub that looked open; warm lights made it inviting as she walked by it. She continued down the street and looked at her phone to see if there were any messages. It was almost dark; she turned around to head back.

"Hey—Sarah!" a voice called out. A door slammed behind it.

Sarah turned around and saw Leif running out from the pub toward her. She smiled at him. "Oh, hey!"

"Hey! What are you up to?" He laughed and smiled at her.

"Just taking a walk-exploring the town a bit." Sarah responded.

"I'm at Walton Pub with my dad and his friends. We just had supper. Want to join us?"

"I was just heading back home actually, it's getting pretty late. But thanks." She smiled.

"Wait here." Leif said and headed back towards the pub, turning back briefly to smile at Sarah one more time.

Sarah waited outside and ran her fingers through her hair. In an instant he ran back outside. "I'll walk you home."

"You don't have to, really," Sarah said. "Go finish supper."

"I already did. It's fine." Leif smiled.

Sarah and Leif started walking back towards Aunt Gale's house. The moon bounced along the sky as the last of the sun disappeared.

"Where do you live?" Sarah asked. She looked up at Leif, he was quite a bit taller and strikingly handsome. Her heart flipped.

"Just back that way." He motioned down the main street. "Close to the cliffs."

Sarah nodded. "So you just moved here too?"

Leif looked down at her, his eyes catching the moon. "Yeah, just a couple weeks before you, actually, because of my dad's work."

"What does your dad do, if you don't mind me asking?" Sarah asked.

"He owns a research company. A mining company," he explained.

"What about your mom?" Sarah inquired.

"My mom's in Norway." He paused and shifted his stance. "My dad is always so focused on his work. I hardly see him. It is the reason that they got a divorce. It was like he forgot about us." Leif rubbed his hands together in the cool air as they walked. "One Christmas, we woke up and couldn't find him anywhere. We searched and searched, tried to call him, asked around, but he couldn't be found. My mom even sent out a rescue team and the police were involved." His hand clenched and he looked down at his shoes.

"Did he come back?" Sarah asked.

"Three days later we found him in a local pub, laughing and joking with his colleagues. Like there was nothing wrong. He just sat there, like he hadn't a care in the world." Leif's voice grew thin and weak.

"I'm so sorry. That's awful," Sarah empathized. She knew what it was like to feel abandoned, but at least her father tried to spend time with her.

"He tried to make up for it in his own way. He promised it would be the best opportunity for me to come here with him. It was his way of trying to spend more time with me, I guess," Leif continued.

"It's hard when your parents aren't how you wish they'd be."

"I don't know why I just told you all that. I don't usually talk about it much." Leif looked into Sarah's eyes. He quickly changed the subject. "So, how about you? You seemed a little frazzled in class today."

"Yeah, I just was having one of those days," Sarah shared. He looked at her, waiting to hear more information. "I couldn't come up with anything good for the assignment."

"How come?"

"I have a hard time remembering anything"—she wasn't sure she wanted to share too much—"before age seven." She immediately felt vulnerable. "My dad and I got in a car accident, ten years ago," she explained. "My dad has amnesia because of it and I … I just deal with horrible, horrible migraines and headaches. My vision was affected and my memory too." Sarah paused. "So that's why it's hard for me to remember that far back."

"That's gotta be tough," Leif said. "You said that your memory was of painting. Do you still paint?"

She looked at him quizzically. "Not really." She wasn't sure why he was being so attentive. Sarah looked down and immediately noticed a ring on Leif's hand. It was black and it had a symbol on it that resembled the keys on the necklace her father was looking for. "That's a cool ring."

Leif looked down at it, then back at her. "Oh, thanks. My dad gave it to me."

"What is it for?" Sarah asked. "The symbol on it."

"It's just a family heirloom. Passed down to me." He smiled.

They were near the pond now, Aunt Gale's house nearby. "It's nice to hang out with someone my own age for once."

"What do you mean?" Sarah asked. "Haven't you met some new friends from school yet?"

"Some I guess. I'm only a couple weeks ahead of you." He laughed. "Moving here meant all my friends are left behind, so I just hang out with my dad and his colleagues. I think they forget what it's like to be my age sometimes. They are pretty focused with their work."

"Well, I'm glad you moved here." She felt awkward suddenly and stepped away. "Gale's probably wondering where I am." Sarah turned toward him. "I'll see you tomorrow?"

"Definitely. See you."

She ran up the road and turned to see Leif walking back down toward the main street. His ring was a curious thing; she could have sworn it was the same symbol that was on the necklace her father was looking for, and the same keys that she drew. She shook away the thought, trying to ignore all the strange connections. At least she had one friend in this new place.

Sarah walked into the house.

"Gale?" She peered into the office but Gale wasn't in there. There was a map opened across the desk of what looked to be Walton. There were circled areas that were labeled: one was designated "pond" and "gazebo," and another said "house" and "forest entrance to headquarters."

Just then, Gale entered the office, startling Sarah. "I see you've found my office. Did you just get in from your walk?"

Gale casually moved toward the desk and rolled up the map. "I was wondering where you went."

"Oh, sorry to barge in here, I was just coming in to say goodnight to you." Sarah walked toward the kitchen.

"And look through my work?" she said with a hint of a smile.

"No, I just noticed it, I wasn't looking through anything."

"It's fine. Goodnight, then." She held the map and thoughtfully opened the drawer to her desk. "Walton really isn't quite what you'd expect, I'll tell you that much."

"What do you mean?"

"The map." Gale searched Sarah's face. "Never mind. Don't worry. Surely you'll find that out very, very soon."

Sarah still didn't know what she meant, but thought it best not to inquire further. "Goodnight, Gale."

"Goodnight then." Gale said abruptly. "There's some mint tea in the pot out there if you'd like some."

"Thanks," Sarah replied. "Goodnight."

She looked back at Gale, and saw her put the map into the drawer and sit down on the chair.

Sarah considered going back into the office to see if Gale was all right, but then saw her take out her phone to make a call.

Walton not what she expected? What else was new? It wasn't surprising, but she didn't know what her aunt was referring to. All she saw was that certain places within Walton were circled on the map, and they were all surrounding Gale's property. She couldn't figure out what was so crazy about that. She ran up the stairs and went into her room. The key stayed in her hoodie pocket. Hanging up her hoodie, she saw it glowing softly from within.

CHAPTER 8

The morning light streamed through the windows of the front door as she ran down the stairs. Gale wasn't in the kitchen but there was evidence of her being awake, as the kettle was still steaming. If she was in her office again, Sarah didn't want to disturb her, especially after yesterday's map discussion. Getting to know Gale wasn't her top priority; getting back to Maine over the next weekend was what she wanted to focus on. Sarah grabbed a muffin from a plate on the table and decided to take the trail to school.

The forest pathway was winding and fairly level, great terrain for running. Every time she entered a forest she felt as though the trees held secrets and invited her to find them out. The shimmering lights were still there, just like the forest by her house in Maine. Was it a coincidence that they were here, too? There was no reason to think that she was the only one to ever see the lights.

There was a beautiful lake past some trees to her right and the pathway ran parallel to it. Someone was in a canoe in the middle of the lake and there were cabins lining the edge on the other side. The water was dazzling in the fall sunlight and the air smelled of rich pine and tree wax. The forest to her left was thick and packed with trees. As she walked, she pondered about the weekend and being able to stay with Stina's family. She hoped there was a way to get to the pawn-shop to see if the necklace was there, so that she could bring it to her dad.

Shortly into her walk, Sarah could feel the familiar headache starting up. She breathed in heavily, and as she exhaled, the glimmering air particles in between the branches of the trees seemed to be swirling closer. She tried brushing them away, like she was swatting at a fly. The headaches had often happened to her in the forest in Augusta and now they were happening here, too. She pressed on, trying to rush her way through so that the headache would go away. The shimmering air particles looked brighter and were more apparent. Not again, she thought.

She looked at the lake and it appeared to be covered with sparkles. The shimmering between the tree branches swirled and twirled faster, and the wind grew. The wind was so strong that it forced Sarah to crouch down on the path. She closed her eyes again, shielding them from the dust. A faint sound like thunder accompanied the wind. As quickly as it began, it stopped and there was a peaceful silence.

She opened her eyes and saw it. Another glimmering key. It was just like the first one that she'd found. She looked around carefully before picking it up. She remembered that the other key was still in her pocket. She quickly unzipped the pocket and took it out. They were almost identical. Both were golden in color and had intricate designs. They looked like antiques, and there was some sort of gem at the top of each of them, one red and one yellow.

"Why am I finding these?" Sarah whispered. There was

another rumble in the sky above her, but the sky was blue, it didn't look like it would rain.

As if answering her question, the glimmering lights fell before her, lacing the keys. It felt like the keys were warmer.

"Hello? Did anyone lose this?" Sarah looked around. Did finding these keys mean anything at all?

Nothing, her inner voice told her. It sounded like Grandfather's. *It means nothing.* The stupid accident caused this, made her see all these strange lights and weird stuff. A part of her wanted to throw the keys into the lake and forget about them. But she decided against it.

In all reality, maybe someone had lost their keys, and she could return them to a nearby store or a lost-and-found somewhere. But it was too random. She'd found one back in Augusta, Maine, and now she'd found one in Walton. She zipped them into the pocket of her hoodie, brushed off her knees as she stood up, and kept walking. Sarah tried to keep them out of her mind. As she left the densely forested area, the headache subsided.

She continued following the trail, trusting it would lead to the school. And when it did, a wave of relief flooded over her. She heard some voices up ahead in the field in front of the school and as she exited the woods, she saw Leif sitting on a rusty picnic table, the paint on it peeling. He was listening to his music, but as he noticed Sarah, he looked up and pulled his earphones out.

"Sarah!" He smiled and jumped down from the table.

She was surprised to see him there, but waved. "How's it going?"

"Good! It was good to see you last night," Leif said, walking towards her.

Sarah laughed. "Yeah, it was. What are you doing waiting here? You'll be late for school."

Leif didn't seem worried. "If I'm late, I'm late. I thought you might take the trail."

She looked back at the trail and felt the keys in her jacket. A part of her wanted to show Leif what she had found, but she decided against it.

"So, you moved in with your aunt?"

"Yeah. How did you know that?"

"Word travels fast." He smiled at her as they walked across the field toward the school.

"Yeah …my dad is …" She paused, refraining from spilling out too much information about her life. "My dad's been busy. So, I had to move." She knew it sounded vague but made no effort to add anything else. She had been surprised at how open Leif was yesterday, but she wasn't sure she wanted to get further into the intricacies of her life with him. "It's a bit complicated."

"I know 'complicated'," he replied.

She could hear the subtle accent in his voice. "So, you're Norwegian." Sarah searched for something else to say. "You speak really great English."

He laughed back. "English is the second language in Norway. We all learn it in school, and we all speak it almost as good as Norwegian," Leif explained.

"Can I hear something in your language?" Sarah asked with a slight smile.

Leif laughed. "I guess so." He paused, thinking about what to say. He then cleared his throat, looking up, and said in a smooth voice, *"Du er vakker og interessant."*

Sarah had to admit, he was very attractive, and the fact that he spoke another language made him even more appealing.

"What does it mean?" Sarah inquired, trying not to smile. The bell rang, and the students were hustling inside.

He smiled, and shrugged his shoulders, backing up

towards the door. "It's a mystery! Going to have to wait until next time." He smiled sweetly.

They had English class first thing. The girl she had seen him talking to after school yesterday was sitting in the back row and had obviously hoped that he would sit beside her. Her eyes followed him to his desk.

Mrs. Lee smiled at Sarah as she entered the room. "Welcome!"

Sarah greeted the teacher and then sat in the same spot at the front of the class, next to Tindra and Christina. Christina was too busy speed texting and chewing gum to greet Sarah, but Tindra welcomed her with a happy smile. "Hey, Sarah. Welcome to your second day at Walton High."

Sarah laughed, "Yeah, thanks." She took out her notebook.

"I just can't wait to be done with high school, to move on, to see the world," Tindra beamed.

"Yeah, I know what you mean. I just want this year to go by fast," Sarah said, pleased to have something in common with her new friend.

The teacher stood up from her desk and the class began to quiet down. "OK, everyone. Yesterday, we left off with a question, 'What is the earliest memory that you have?'" She looked around the class and then lightly laughed. "And some of yours were interesting, to say the least."

Everyone turned to look at Zack.

He nodded and said, "What can I say?"

"It truly is amazing what the brain can remember. I would say my earliest memory was when I was three. I was climbing a small tree in the backyard with the help of my grandfather. He was watching me as I stood on a branch," Mrs. Lee shared.

The students were listening intently.

"Our first project within our creative writing unit is to create a piece of art, in the form of writing, that portrays your earliest memory. I want you to express the feelings that you remember, whether happy or sad. Maybe there are colors you remember. Smells."

Sarah shifted in her seat. She looked back at Leif who glanced at her and smiled.

Why did this assignment have to be about memories, when her memory was the very thing that stifled her, that confused her? How could anyone remember that far back?

Mrs. Lee continued, "I want you to take your audience on a journey to your memory." She paused and began passing out the assignment instructions. "Let the reader go into your writing, as if it is a portal." Mrs. Lee looked right at Sarah as she spoke, passing her the sheet. "Let your words take them on a journey." She continued past, and Tindra eagerly reached for the sheet.

It was as if Mrs. Lee's words had punched Sarah in her brain. Her thoughts were slower, and the fuzzy feeling came back. A sharp headache started up again and Sarah's eyes started watering. Not now, not now, Sarah pleaded to herself.

"Sarah, are you OK?" Tindra was leaning from her desk, but before she got an answer, Sarah shot up, her hand on her head and walked out the door, leaving the class looking at each other in confusion. Mrs. Lee handed the last of the pages out.

Tindra spoke up. "She was breathing heavily and looked like she was going to pass out. Maybe I should check on her."

"Yes, please, go ahead." Mrs. Lee gave permission.

Tindra disappeared around the corner. Sarah was in the hallway on her hands and knees. Tindra ran over to her.

"Sarah are you OK? The washrooms are back there."

After a moment, Sarah sat up, resting her back against the locker. "I'm sorry." Her face was all sweaty and tears were in the corners of her eyes. "I … I just have these really bad migraines on occasion. All this talk about memories, it's … it's exhausting."

"Yeah, I suppose." Tindra searched for something else to say. "Why don't you just go home? I can pick up homework for you."

"Thanks. But my home is eight hours away. This is just a temporary place that I am staying in." She looked at Tindra who was kneeling beside her, full of concern. "I, of course, had no choice in the matter."

"That sounds pretty bad," Tindra sympathized. "Seriously though, you need some water. Let's go to the fountain."

Sarah reluctantly stood up. Other students stared at her as they walked by. A surge of weakness came over her and she almost collapsed again, but Tindra helped her stand by holding her arm.

She took several deep breaths. "It's so weird. I did not think I'd have one of these episodes again." She drank some water. "Usually they're lighter headaches, but consistent. It happened when I went into the forest trail, on the way to school, but I thought it was over."

Tindra listened and then spoke up again. "So, do you want to go back to class?"

"I can try," Sarah said.

They went back into the classroom. Leif looked at Sarah and mouthed, "Are you OK?"

She nodded at him.

"Are you all right, Sarah?" Mrs. Lee looked worried. "If you need to take the day to rest, I can understand."

"I'm fine. I'll be fine." Sarah looked down at the page and blinked a couple times. The page that had been white was now blue and moving like a wave. She dropped the paper, and it regained its normal shape. "I just have a really bad headache."

Sarah wanted to tough it out. She didn't want her

episodes to become like her father's. She thought of her dad, alone in his cell, and her heart ached. Looking at the sheet again, she distracted herself with the assignment. She could write a short story, a poem or a song. The second part was the visual representation.

Mrs. Lee stood in the row beside Sarah and said something that wasn't clear. The teacher's face almost morphed slightly, but Sarah knew it was because of the migraine.

Sarah closed her eyes for a few moments and breathed deeply until she started to feel settled again. She felt the keys in her pocket; they were still warm, like when she'd found each one of them in the forest. She quickly took them out of her pocket, trying to hide their glow, and threw them into her bag.

A few minutes later Sarah saw something within her bag move. Her eyes widened. She didn't want to be the subject of attention again. Mrs. Lee was still walking through the aisles and she noticed it too. Sarah cautiously unzipped the bag. The two keys were floating within the confines of the bag. She gasped. They glimmered extra brightly.

She quickly zipped it up again, then saw Mrs. Lee looking at her strangely.

"Um, I think I'd better go," Sarah said to the teacher. She stood up, grabbed her bag, and walked out of the classroom.

Mrs. Lee followed her into the hall. "Sarah, what is in your bag? There's something moving in it."

Sarah didn't answer. She was halfway down the hallway, picking up the pace until she got to the doors.

"Sarah! Please sign out in the office!" Mrs. Lee shouted.

She could hear Leif behind Mrs. Lee in the hall, "Sorry, I have to go too."

"Where do you think you're going?"

Sarah didn't sign out. She ran out the door and away from the school. Her headache was stronger, and the thought of floating keys in her bag was too crazy. She had to have been seeing things. But did Mrs. Lee see it too? Once she was out of the school, she unzipped the bag slowly once again. The keys weren't floating anymore. The accident. It's because of the accident. Her grandfather and father would say the same thing. She zipped it back up.

"Hey! Sarah—what's up?" Leif ran after her. "Are you OK?" He was looking at her bag. Did he see the keys too?

The principal walked out behind them. "Leif? Sarah? What's going on here? Back in class please."

Leif turned around and went back into the school, but Sarah continued walking down the hill toward the town, her mind going over what the keys could mean, and who they could belong to.

Walton was very quaint. There were little stores that lined the downtown streets, the storefronts all squished neatly together. There was a small café across from a grocer that caught her eye, just down the street from the pub that Leif had come out of last night. It had the name "Rosie's" on the sign over the door. She decided to go in. There were two older men chatting near the counter, another man was sitting by the door reading a newspaper. He briefly looked up at Sarah and immediately took a sip of his coffee and resumed reading. A young man who looked to be in his twenties, with long, light blond hair, was leaning on the high table in the window with his earphones in. He glanced at Sarah and held her gaze for a few moments. His eyes were light blue. He clenched his phone in one hand. Sarah noticed a long scar under his left eye, then quickly looked away and walked toward the counter, glancing back briefly to see that the man was still watching her.

"What can I get for you?" A stern woman with her hair tied back waited for Sarah to say something.

"A hot chocolate please." Sarah inspected the colorful

Canadian ten-dollar bill that Gale had given her before handing it over to the woman. Even the money was slightly different here. She felt out of place and she felt suspicious, like people knew that she should be in school. She continued to grasp her backpack as if there was a dangerous monster inside, ready to attack. She tried to relax. She took out her phone and picked up the hot chocolate that was ready for her on the counter. She took a sip of the creamy chocolate drink before placing a lid on the cup.

Her headache was subsiding, but she couldn't bear going back to class. All she wanted to do was rush back to Augusta and see her father and somehow help his case. If it meant finding some necklace that he needed, then she would help him find it.

Who else was going to help him? Her grandfather? Gale? No one cared. She then thought of Leif's ring. Maybe if the ring and the necklace had the same symbol on it, maybe Leif could help. But the thought quickly dissipated. How could Leif have anything to do with her problems?

"A woman named Gale," one of the older men said. He and the man he was talking to both looked like they could be locals. One had a newspaper open in his hands, and the other had a coffee lifted, mid sip. "Moved in just the other day. Strange woman. That house has been empty for a decade, and supposedly it was the first house she saw in the area."

"Well, hopefully she can tidy it up. It's so run down," the other man commented. "Ever since that disappearance in the forest, no one wants to take on that area."

"Jim tried to purchase it a few years back, but for some reason the owner wouldn't take his offer."

"Who owned the house?"

"No one that I know has met him. He's not local."

Sarah's eavesdropping became apparent as she bumped into a table that was directly behind the table and chairs where the men were sitting. They looked at her briefly before going back to their conversation.

A part of her wanted to jump into the conversation and tell them that they were wrong, and that her aunt had always lived there. But what did she know? She'd just met her aunt. Maybe she didn't know the whole story; she didn't know anything about Gale except for what her father had told her.

Sarah swiftly moved toward the door and into the autumn air. Maybe those men were talking about another Gale. What would it matter anyway? She dropped the subject. Sarah continued down the street. A few people were out and about, going in and out of the grocery store. She saw a dock at the end of the main street and decided to walk toward it. The salty air was fresh and invigorating. Hoping her headache would subside, she breathed in deeper.

She quickly pulled her phone from her pocket to message Stina.

"Enjoying your hot chocolate?" A mysterious voice shocked Sarah as she sipped her drink.

She looked behind her and saw the same young man with the long, blond hair who had been in the café, except now he was leaning against a tree. Sarah felt strange that the man had followed her and so she said nothing.

"It truly is the best place in town," he boasted.

Sarah tried to ignore him and continued walking.

"Okay, so it's the only place in town." The man kept pace with Sarah as she walked.

"What do you want?" Sarah stopped and faced him, phone in hand. "You were in the café and now you are following me —can I help you with something?" Sarah was annoyed at this point. The guy needed to back off. He was standing way too close to her for her comfort.

"Oh, I was there, wasn't I? By the way, shouldn't you be in school?" He laughed and stared at her smugly, his hands in the pockets of his long jacket. He then stopped and looked around before whispering, his voice serious, "You're her, right?"

He was tall, his blue eyes were piercing, and he had a well-defined face. The scar under his eye held the sheen from the sun. His fine, long hair blew in the wind.

Sarah ignored him and started walking again, but he continued to talk.

"You're …" he paused, and carefully whispered, "You're the one. You're the next in line, aren't you? Listen, you need to be careful."

She kept going, and the man continued to follow her. "This is why we were sent here. To find you. And … and now you're here in front of me!" His voice sounded excited. "The restoration of the Painter's Keep is closer than ever. I can almost smell it!"

Sarah spun around and faced him. "What are you talking about? I have no idea what any of that means. The Painter's Keep? Leave me alone. You have me mistaken for someone else."

He was caught off guard and must have realized that he had the wrong person. Sarah was puzzled at his questions but turned away again to ignore him.

"You don't know what I am talking about? Surely you know the state of the Startrail, don't you?" the man questioned. He stayed for a few moments in the one spot, perplexed. "But you're different. And tell me, what do you have in your bag then? I can detect the stardust, in you, and certainly in the bag. Stop kidding around."

He looked up at the sky and then back at Sarah. Bewilderment was written all over his face. "We were told that you could be here. That's why we came." She backed away from him slowly. He looked down.

How could he know that there was something in her bag?

He was right about that. *Well, obviously, that's what bags are for, to hold things,* she reasoned. But it seemed like he knew there was something else. Something unusual. Sarah didn't respond, even though she desperately wanted to tell someone about the random keys. She pushed the thought away, telling herself to ignore it, there was nothing more that needed to be explored.

He continued, "Sometimes I can tell certain things about people, and I thought …" He looked back and then upwards. "Never mind. If you change your mind, meet me here tomorrow after school."

Sarah started walking again, thankful to be rid of him. She finally got to the dock and turned to walk out on it, looking back briefly to make sure that the man was gone. What was he talking about, the Painter's Keep? That she was the next in line? Detecting stardust? It all made no sense. She craved something that was real.

The tide was in and the water was slopping against the old wooden pilings that held the dock up. It was rickety, but she walked on it anyway. The waves were getting higher and the wind had started up. Sarah's eyes began to blur. She reasoned that she'd better get back to solid ground and go back to Gale's. The migraine episodes were not over. Waves of nausea crept up on her. Sarah sat down on the creaky dock to regain her balance. A flash of light came over her very briefly and then it went away. And then another flash of light. A vision of starlight dripping from a vase appeared in her mind's eye and then it vanished. Hands that were covered in paint, that were worn, could be seen holding the vase. One of the hands reached out and held three keys. A voice could be heard but it wasn't clear. "Put the keys together to bring new." But then the voice stopped.

Before she could analyze the vision, she regained awareness of herself. She looked at her phone and was shocked to discover that she had blacked out for several hours. Another memory was trying to come back. Or was it a vision? Whatever it was, it had to do with the keys again. It didn't matter, she reasoned with herself. *None of this matters.*

She felt strange and groggy from the vision, she needed to rest and so she decided to walk towards Gale's house hoping that she wouldn't make a big deal about missing school. The door was open, but Gale wasn't home. Sarah checked each room, including her aunt's office. The drawer that had the map in it was shut and everything was tidy. She noticed that the office was like the rest of the house—there wasn't much in it. Either Gale was very minimalistic, or the people at the coffee shop were right about her just moving in. The living room was simply furnished. One couch, a chair, a coffee table. There was no TV. She walked into the kitchen and investigated the drawers. One had cutlery in it, but the others were empty. Sarah felt uneasy, but she reminded herself that social workers were professionals, and they wouldn't just lie about who Gale is. *Neither would your father, who loves you,* she said to herself.

"Gale?" Sarah called out. No answer. Her vehicle wasn't in the driveway either. Sarah went up to her room and took out the notebook that she had started to use as a journal. It would have to do, since her own journal was still missing. She reflected on the drawing that she had made in class of the keys and then started writing under it.

So strange, Sarah began to write, *here I am in a new town, nobody who really knows me, and who is really going to care about my well-being. I had a migraine today that turned into a full-on vision, if you want to call it that. Plus, I found 2 keys that look identical, and they seem to have some strange power.*

Then she wrote into words what she had seen, in the form of a poem. It's what she often did, to get straight to the point. At least she would understand this.

Blue starlight flow
Pouring from the glassy vase
Hands that know a timeless fate
White light flashing, another place
Memory bleak but mind
Remembering
Blue starlight flow

I saw hands that were covered in paint, holding out keys.
Keys.

She looked back at the drawing of the keys. *I need to find the necklace Dad was talking about, to see if it's anything real,* she wrote next. Maybe it could help his case, maybe not. *I guess I just miss Dad, and I miss who he really is, and I miss who I was. Whoever that was.*

SARAH HAD FALLEN ASLEEP, ANOTHER COUPLE HOURS HAD passed, and it was getting darker. She stood up quickly and looked out the window, Gale's vehicle was still gone. There was enough evening light to go for a run. Maybe that strange man knew something about the keys. He could have an explanation. But why? Why did she find them in the first place? She changed into her running clothes, left the keys in the bag in her room, and ran outside and into the trails.

Vibrant evergreens grazed her arms as she ran through the narrow entrance. As usual, the slight shimmer between the branches was still there, hovering and dancing around. The leaves on the silver birch trees were yellow and sparse. To her astonishment, a couple of yards into the forest, two keys suddenly appeared in front of her feet. Sarah stopped and picked them up. Were they the same ones? It looked like it, but how did they get back into the forest? She swiftly walked back toward the house. Gale's car was still not there. She ran up the stairs, into her room, and grabbed her backpack. She unzipped the bag and gasped. The keys weren't inside.

She looked at the two keys in her hand. Could it be them? How could they have got to the forest on their own? Did Gale go in there and take them and put them in the forest? Sarah thought of a bunch of possibilities, none of which made sense. Or was her mind playing tricks on her again? But she was holding the physical keys in her hand, she couldn't deny it. She put them back in the bag and left them. She then walked out of the house again before starting to run toward the trails. And there they were, the keys. Right in front of her. The sun was resting on the horizon, the soft evening glow making the gems on the keys glisten.

Sarah felt angry. She grabbed the keys and looked around. The quietness of the forest seemed to watch her every move. She looked up to the sky, up at the tops of the trees, and shouted, "What do you want with me?" She threw the keys into the bushes. She didn't want them; she didn't need them. She hated how it brought more confusion upon her. They landed on a patch of moss by some evergreens. Sarah looked at them for a few seconds and then took off in a sprint down the trail. Anger and confusion turned into tears of loneliness. She missed her dad, she missed her old life, she missed what was before. Before the accident. Whatever that was, she missed it. "I don't care, I don't care. I don't want to be confused, I just …"

She ran and ran, tears fogging up her eyes. A few leaves were quietly dropping over her head. The evening light was so soft and subtle. It was like an enchanted land, far away from the dismal and mundane reality. She stopped suddenly, the blur in her eyes from the tears made it hard to see. She crouched down and sobbed. It wasn't the keys, it wasn't the new school. It was the fact that her dad was stuck in prison with no one to help him, no one to help his case. All the frustrations of the day were piling up and over top of the one thing that broke her heart. Her father was alone in jail. The trickery of her eyes and the angst of the confusion she felt gnawed at her.

One leaf fell directly in front of her, a precise maple leaf, perfectly red all over. The only red one, she noticed. The rest of the leaves on the tree above her or on the ground were yellow. The evening light was sparse now, making it hard to see very much color. The ache in her head stabbed; she knew as soon as she looked at the shimmering lights, she would feel it. She ignored the headache and picked up the red leaf. She inspected it; it was flawlessly red in color, and there were no scratches or tears on the surface. Sarah flipped it over and looked at the other side. Her eyes widened. The leaf appeared to be see-through, or like a mirror. She gasped and let go of it, but then curiosity led her to pick it up again. As she held it, she noticed that it was pulling out of her grip, as if the wind was blowing it around, making it hard to grasp. She looked closer at the see-through side of the leaf. She could almost put her finger right into it, but when she tried, the leaf itself blocked her. It felt just like a normal leaf again, and yet it was like a peephole into another place.

"What is this?" she whispered to herself.

Her heart beating faster, she looked around as if worried someone would see her in this amazed state. She looked at the leaf again. All she could see was a faint light glimmering within it. Was there something in there, in the other place, within the leaf? She breathed in and out, trying to keep quiet, as if her very breath would disrupt this fantastical moment. It was completely impossible, yet mesmerizing. She looked up, making sure that no one else was around. She would look ridiculous staring at a leaf. Looking back down, it was as if time stopped. She could have sworn that she saw something move within the mirrored area. Something blinked. It was an eye. An eye was looking through the leaf back at her. Sarah immediately shrieked, fell backwards and dropped the leaf.

"What is this?" she said out loud. The leaf lay there on the ground in the middle of the empty trail. "Who's there?" She felt like she had to say it, half expecting a magician to jump out of the bushes and say, "Surprise!" There was no sound. She bent down and slowly touched the leaf again, as if it was scalding hot. She brought her hand up. Then she carefully reached back down and grabbed the stem with her fingers. She flipped it over, expecting to see the eye again, but it was gone. The mirror, the eye, even the force that the leaf seemed to have before, were gone.

Questions flooded her mind. She felt half-embarrassed that she had even looked at the leaf again. She looked around the thick, forested area. The trees stood tall, swaying in the silence, wafting in the cool wind. It felt like they were laughing at her, watching her in this crazy moment of time. There was something very strange about this forest, just like there was something odd about her forest back in Augusta. Was there a connection? This was the only other forest she had seen that displayed the shimmering lights like the ones in Augusta. But she had never before seen whatever she saw in the leaf. Ever. She stood up quickly, trying to ignore the fear that tore at her. She decided to head back. Gale would be wondering where she was. That is, if Gale was back home yet. Maybe it was just her imagination. But was that all it was, or was any of it real?

I touched the leaf with my hands, she reasoned, and I saw it with my own eyes. As she turned back toward the house, there they were. The two keys. Like lost puppies, they were waiting for her. Like they belonged to her.

"Who's there?" Sarah shouted. Maybe someone was playing a trick on her. "Who put these here? Gale?"

There was no answer. She walked around the keys and, ignoring the fear, started running back toward the house. But within moments, the keys showed up in front of her. Again, and again, she tried to walk away from them, but they kept appearing. She looked up at the evening sky, exhaustion taking over. She slowly picked up the keys and zipped them into her pocket. For now, she'd keep them. The strange keys that seemed to claim her. There was no point in analyzing any further. The migraines were too painful. Maybe these keys were just hallucinations, like what her dad experienced. And now the eye in the leaf. What did it all mean? Sarah felt like someone was watching and waiting for her to do something.

Maybe the keys were magic, or maybe they had some sort of magnetic property that caused them to follow her around. Both of those reasons made no logical sense. The stupid accident. It was the stupid accident that made her have all these visions, hallucinations, and now seeing strange things that followed her. Maybe jail was next for her.

Gale's car was pulling into the driveway. Sarah was just about to run into the house but noticed a man exiting the passenger's side of the car. She watched and waited behind a shed.

"She wasn't there when I left, so we'll see." Gale's whisper carried in the night air.

The man followed Gale into the house. He was tall, with well-coiffed hair.

"We have to move fast; these transitions are usually seamless, but with her state of mind …" The man's voice faltered. "Has she discovered any of them yet?"

"She carries so much with her already, but she has no clue. I think she has found one. I think she has it with her."

Sarah stood behind the shed in the yard, listening carefully.

"Keep watch. Once she finds them, that's when we move in. Not until she finds them. If they are being sent to her, we must wait until they all are sent."

"How they have been sent is something that takes the mind of a master," Gale considered.

Gale walked into the house. The man walked in behind her.

Sarah slowly walked back as well, hoping she wouldn't have to discuss anything with them. She walked in and ran up the stairs.

"Sarah?" Gale shouted from the living room. "You were out late."

"Yeah, I went for a run." Sarah paused on the stairs, hoping they wouldn't ask any more questions.

The man who was with Gale was caught off guard. He looked up at Sarah from the couch he was sitting on.

"Hi there," he said, nodding toward her.

"Sarah, this is my friend Henrikson. We were just getting back from the restaurant."

Sarah smiled. "Nice to meet you." He seemed a lot younger than Gale. She wondered how they knew each other.

"If you don't mind, I think I'll head to bed," Sarah excused herself.

"Yes, of course," Gale said.

She walked up the stairs, leaving Gale and her guest silent in the living room. Her journal was still on her bed. She placed it on her bedside table. Soft chatter could be heard downstairs. If Gale was talking to her friend about Sarah finding things, maybe the keys were supposed to be found. The question was, why?

CHAPTER 9

The prison cell wall was cool against Stanley Carlson's back as he leaned against it. He was about to be taken to the prison doctor, who would give him his dose of medication. These meds would keep him balanced and minimize his seizures and migraines. He felt like he was doing better; he wasn't consumed by the need to find what he was looking for. He did, however, keep having those dreams, the same ones, about a woman with ash-colored hair holding out a necklace to him. Behind her was a glass countertop that contained trinkets, antiques, and a name he knew, a name of a shop. The shop was Holden's Pawnshop. He could never see her face, but he knew she was beautiful. Her hands were delicately holding the silver chain that held a unique-looking pendant. It was a locket that had a crimson jewel on the front of it, and within, it contained a force that Stanley knew was powerful. He looked away every time the woman opened it. Then the dream would be over. That's why he was consumed with that photo, and why he gave it to Sarah. His father was wearing the necklace. Why was he wearing it and why hadn't Stanley noticed it before?

It was as if new memories started to come back when he looked at the picture.

For the past ten years, Stanley remembered having dreams or visions. They were minimal at first, but every year or so, they got worse, along with the amnesia that was the cause of them. His memory had been badly affected by the accident. He couldn't remember anything past ten years ago. At least, the memories he could remember weren't consistent with his reality. It was the collision that brought everything on. The last ten years, working at the factory, shipping off sporting goods, was very routine and his condition didn't hinder him, but as it got worse, his performance at work dwindled. Once, he had tried to get a resume together to apply for another job, but he couldn't remember past the time when he'd started at the factory. It became too much of a hassle to explain his condition to any potential employers, so he just stayed at the same job, living the same life that he knew.

But the visions got worse, especially when he didn't take his medication, and this latest one had gotten him into huge trouble, keeping him from Sarah. His heart sank and ached at the thought of disappointing his daughter. She was always there for him, helping him out when she should be focused on just being a kid. He was glad he'd had his dad there to keep him company for five of those years, when he lived with them. The last five years, with him living in the seniors' home, made him seem more distant.

Stanley was able to have his own cell for medical reasons. The prison guard opened the cell door and Stanley followed him to the doctor's office. Other prisoners made rude calls and shouted after them as they passed.

The doctor was a middle-aged man. He was always kind and knowledgeable about Stanley's situation, and always knew the dosage that he should take.

"Good afternoon, Mr. Carlson. Take a seat." Doctor Yun motioned for him to sit on the plush seat, one of the highlights of going to see the doctor.

"I haven't had any severe headaches in the last week. I've been taking my medication at dinner; the meal guard gives it to me." Stanley felt uneasy telling Dr. Yun about his visions, but he had mentioned it before and felt he had to mention it again. "But …"

Dr. Yun looked up from his notes.

Stanley continued, "I feel like I should see a psychiatrist. I keep having the same dreams, and whenever I have a seizure —the last one was over a week ago, as you know—I have a vision of the same thing."

"Interesting," Dr. Yun noted. "But it's normal to have these things happen. When your brain is unconscious, you are likely to have all sorts of hallucinations or strange visions. It happens to people."

Stanley felt like relief should have come with that explanation, but he couldn't help but think that there was more to his visions and dreams. "I feel like I am …" He stopped and looked at the floor.

Dr. Yun interjected, "Going crazy?"

Stanley looked up and nodded. He felt like what he was seeing were not hallucinations but very real, like memories. Why? He didn't know. But maybe this was how severe mental health situations got started.

"The fact that you feel like you are going crazy shows that you aren't going crazy." Dr. Yun spun around on his chair, back to his notes, before leaning back to say, "If you were crazy, we would not be having this discussion, about going crazy."

Stanley felt that it made sense. "The reason I robbed that store was because of one of the visions."

Dr. Yun paused. "And we all make mistakes. Yours,

however, happened to be against the law and it harmed someone else."

"That wasn't my fault. I didn't hurt that person." Stanley was getting riled up and as he stood up in anger, the security guards came to intervene.

"It's okay, he'll be fine." The doctor brushed the security guards away. There was a pause. Stanley took a deep breath and sat down.

"Listen, Stanley. Maybe I believe you, maybe I don't. It is not up to me to decide. But what I can say is that you must hope for some sort of resolution to this. Maybe there will be more evidence in your favor. I hope that what you believe is correct." He smiled.

"My daughter must think the worst of me. Now she's forced to finish school in another town. Another country." Stanley sighed, sitting back down.

"Well, visitation is coming up, did you not tell me that last week?" Dr Yun asked.

"Yes, yes I did. She should be here sometime this weekend." The relief he wished for suddenly flooded over him. He could see his daughter. "Dr. Yun, I feel like I may be able to decrease my medication."

Dr. Yun just looked at him for a moment then stated, "We can't do that. Your condition can cause harm to you, and it can cause harm to others if you have an episode near them. You have been in my care for almost a month. I'd like to keep you on this stuff for a while longer, then we can do some trial and error with dosage."

Stanley knew the doctor was right, he knew that he needed the medication to be safe, but he didn't want to be safe. Deep down, he wanted to go back to the vision, to see what else he would discover, and without the medication he was able to do that. It's not like he was going to rob any stores around here. He was locked up. He was safe in that way.

"Glad to hear that you have not had any headaches. Your last seizure was over a week ago and we hope for no more in the future. So, you can take your first dose with me and I'll inform the meal guard that you have already taken it."

"Thanks." He took the pill. "See you next week."

The guard walked him back to his cell and he settled in again. He turned his back to the cell door and spat. The skin of the capsule was dissolving but he got it out just in time. Maybe being "crazy" means finding answers, he thought. He picked up a book and turned to the page that he had written in last. It was about his latest vision. The necklace, the ashy hair, and the pawnshop. He put down the date and time that he had spat out his medication, and put the book back under his mattress. He'd write in it when he had something of worth to write.

CHAPTER 10

The bell had already gone and everyone was in class.

Phys ed class took place outside; Sarah learned that they were halfway through the cross-country unit. She was about to leave her backpack in the locker when she remembered the keys that continually followed her. Sarah opened her backpack carefully and looked down the hall, making sure no one was around. The keys glistened.

What are you? she thought to herself. *Why did I find you?*

Grabbing the keys and zipping them into the pocket of her sweater, she ran outside to join the others. Tindra was sitting in the field with the class.

"You seem like the running type," Tindra said as Sarah sat down beside her. "Are you going to join the cross-country team?"

"Yeah, maybe," Sarah's mind was on the keys; she felt like she needed to tell someone about what she'd found. "Hey Tindra, look at this." She unzipped her pocket and took out one of the keys. "I found this in the forest over there."

"Wow, maybe someone lost it? It's so unique looking," Tindra observed. "What are you going to do with it?"

"There's not just one," Sarah said, "There's …"

They were interrupted by Christina who sauntered over to join them.

"So, are you going to join the running club? It's Tuesday and Thursday after school," Christina explained. "It's not really my type of sport, but I might do it. You know, to keep in shape."

Sarah noticed Leif wandering out onto the field with some of the guys. She put the key back into her pocket and zipped it up.

"I might. I did cross-country at my other school and was part of a track team," Sarah responded.

"It would be fun if we all joined," Tindra added.

"Hey, Sarah," Leif greeted her as he walked past the others.

"Hey." Sarah smiled back and then she turned back to Tindra and Christina.

"Oh, Leif seems to like you," Christina noted mid gum-chew. "He's a new student too, just got here two weeks ago."

Tindra responded, "Yeah, Sarah, you should totally go for him."

Sarah wanted to ignore their comments, but let the thought linger in her mind a while. Although she liked Leif's company, she didn't want to get too connected to this school. All her friends were in Augusta. And even though it was eight hours away, she was determined to get there every weekend. The long weekend was coming up and she could stay longer if she wanted.

"Have you ever been in those woods that are way behind the school?" Sarah asked while stretching. "There's a trail in them."

Christina and Tindra looked at each other. "Yeah, it's

creepy in there. I went in once for a dare and didn't make it ten yards in," Tindra said and laughed. "Is that where you found the …"

Sarah quickly cut Tindra off, she felt hesitant about revealing what she had found to Christina or anyone else. For a moment, she even regretted telling Tindra about the keys. She was starting to feel protective over them, but she didn't understand why.

"It's a shortcut from my aunt's house to get to school," Sarah said, feeling out the topic, seeing if they would spill more information.

"Well, you're brave. I heard that someone went missing in there," Christina piped up. "Is your aunt the one that just moved into that house on the hill?"

Sarah was caught off guard.

"She didn't 'just' move there," she said.

"I heard she just moved to Walton. It was an empty house for years," Tindra added.

Sarah was about to respond but the teacher started shouting at them to come together and start stretching.

The men in the coffee shop must have been right about Gale. But if she'd just moved to Walton, where did she come from? Sarah was being kept in the dark. She felt bad for not making an effort to get to know this new aunt of hers, but then, Gale wasn't making an effort either.

Sarah longed to leave for Augusta today. Even just being in the same city as her father seemed like it might help. She wished she was a lawyer, an investigator, or that she knew some good ones.

Sarah took a deep breath, aiming to tuck her worries somewhere far away in the caverns of her mind. She looked back to see Leif stretching and getting ready for the class. He glanced up at Sarah. He was moving towards her but Keira, the girl who always seemed to be around Leif, was stretching next to him and started talking to him. The teacher, Mr. Andrews, got their attention. He gave them the plan for the day and asked for everyone to sign up for the cross-country race that was two weeks from now. Training would begin after the long weekend. The class started the 3 kilometre run, which Sarah quickly converted to being roughly two-miles. They were to run around the field, through a couple of neighborhoods, around the school, and then back past the forest with the trails, running along the outside of it. Sarah was ahead of the pack from the beginning. Christina fell behind quite quickly, and Tindra kept up with Sarah for a bit, but Sarah continued to move ahead. It felt good to stretch out her legs; her muscles thanked her at every stride. She heard someone coming up behind her, glanced to the right, and it was Leif.

"Hey," he said. Leif had a good stride. As he ran up beside her, she realized how tall he really was. His dark hair bounced on top of his head. "You're fast!"

Sarah laughed. "So are you."

"Are you going to do the race in a couple weeks?" Leif inquired.

"I might," Sarah stated. She glanced back and noticed that Keira was fifty yards behind them. Her face looked strained as she ran.

"Sarah, are you OK from yesterday? I realized I didn't get your number, so I couldn't call you." Leif smiled.

"Yeah, it's the migraines. Sometimes they come back at different times."

"The accident." Leif made the connection. "I would have come with you but the principal …"

"It's OK."

They both ran for a little while without talking.

"What are you up to this weekend?" asked Leif, a little out

of breath. "I heard that Rocco is having a party. Maybe you'd like to come with me?"

She was surprised to feel a little upset that she already had plans to go home.

"Sounds fun. But I'm going home this weekend. I've decided to go home every weekend." She realized that her reply may have sounded like she was shutting him down, but she made no effort to fix it.

"Oh?" Leif looked disappointed.

"Sorry, that sounded like I didn't want to go to the party. I would like to, with you. But home is all the way in Augusta, Maine," Sarah answered.

Leif looked surprised. "Right."

She saw that they were almost back where they started. A couple of other runners were close behind them. "Let's pick up the pace."

Leif laughed nervously and smiled. "Uh, OK."

Sarah noticed he was breathing a little heavy. She ran off ahead of him, causing him to fall behind, but to Sarah's surprise he found a surge of energy and both raced nose to nose to where their teacher stood at the finish line.

They laughed and gave each other a high five. Three minutes later Keira ran across the finish line, totally red in the face. She keeled over, her hands on her knees.

"Wow, good times for both of you. I hope you two join the cross-country team." Mr. Andrews laughed as he recorded their times in his notes.

Keira walked up to Leif with some of her friends. "Good run, Leif," she said, as she fixed her ponytail. She didn't seem to be fazed by Sarah at all, and didn't acknowledge her.

"Thanks, Keira." He smiled. She waited around a bit but then slowly walked away with her friends.

As they stretched out and had their water, Sarah looked

over to the forest where the trail was. She could still see the lights shimmer above the trees. Just like in Augusta. She longed to share what she saw with people, to be able to talk about it, but refrained. Alone with her thoughts she would remain.

Leif was looking at her sweater. She had her pocket unzipped and the keys were glowing from within.

"What's that?" The ring on his finger glistened in the sun as he pointed to her pocket.

"Nothing. Just something I found," Sarah replied. She zipped up her sweater pocket and smiled at Leif. Leif stared at her as if he was about to say something, but Sarah turned to catch up with Tindra and Christina, leaving Leif to walk by himself. She kicked herself for not walking back with him, but she didn't want him to inquire about the keys.

The students walked into the school to change and get ready for their next class.

There is more, there is more. Her dad's words echoed in her mind. Maybe there was more behind everything that could be seen. Maybe she was on the cusp of discovering something great, but what would be the point if no one else could see it or understand?

There had to be more. *The keys.* She placed her hand over them in her pocket. *The strange keys.* Then there was the leaf with the eye looking out from it. Was there a connection? She pushed the thoughts away. Grandfather's voice reminded her: *the amnesia, the accident. You must move on.* The afternoon breezed by, another school day complete.

Sarah walked toward the back doors. Leif ran up to her. "Hey, Sarah. Want to go grab some food or something?"

She thought about the strange man she had met yesterday. How he had told her to meet him at the dock this afternoon if she wanted to talk to him. Maybe meeting with him wasn't the right thing to do, even though he might be able to explain the keys. "Yeah, sure, that works."

"Cool. It would be good to check out the town," Leif said.

"There is not much to explore." Tindra must have over-heard their conversation and was laughing. "I can show you the good spots. I don't have dance today, anyway."

Leif smiled at Tindra and then at Sarah. "Yeah sure, why not."

"That would be nice. What kind of dance do you do?" Sarah inquired.

"Ballet, jazz, and basically everything else. I was born a dancer, you could say." Tindra beamed and they walked out the doors. "It really is a small town, Sarah. Everyone knows everybody, and the only nice thing about the place is the ocean. Sometimes you can see whales in the distance, or dolphins." Tindra glanced at Leif.

"That's how everyone knows about my aunt," Sarah replied. "It would have been great to know more about her before I moved in."

"Yeah, well, people are always aware of any new neigh-bors or visitors," Tindra said. "Like I said, the town is small."

Sarah didn't say anything.

They wandered from the school down the pathway that led to the main street. The bright sign of the café came into view.

"So, this is the only café, and then across the street there is a grocery store, the only one in town, really. And, next to it is the library. Next to the library is the art gallery, then there is the pub over there, and then after that, there's the mechan-ic," Tindra explained. She took a breath and exhaled loudly. "And that's pretty much it."

Leif's hands were in his jacket pockets as he looked around. The chill in the air allowed his breath to be seen.

Sarah's eyes lit up. "Art gallery?" She could get her supplies from there.

"Yes! My family owns it," Tindra said. "You said that you paint, right?'

Sarah started to reply, but Tindra interrupted while jingling change that was in her pocket. "Do you guys want to get hot chocolate?"

There were a couple of other students in the café, chatting and drinking sweet drinks with whipped cream. Leif opened the door for Tindra and Sarah. Tindra smiled at the gesture. Sarah briefly looked down the street to see if the man was at the dock. It was past 3:00 p.m. and she was curious if he would be there. They were about to walk up to the counter when Sarah spotted the tall man through the window, walking across the street from the café. His long, ashy-colored hair blew back in the wind. He was wearing a long black jacket. A chain with a large pendant on it sparkled in the sunlight. He looked like he was in a rush and was busy texting someone on his phone.

"Actually, let's skip the hot chocolate." Sarah hesitated; her eyes remained glued on the man.

"Wait, why?" Tindra whirled around after her. Leif was watching Sarah intently, he walked with her to the café door. She was watching through the glass to see where the man was going.

"What are you looking at?" Leif stood behind her, looking out the window. Tindra followed along impatiently.

"That guy followed me yesterday," Sarah whispered, and pointed out the man who was nearing the gallery.

"Why? Oh my goodness, that's creepy. I've never seen him before," Tindra said.

"Followed you? Did he say anything?" Leif looked at Sarah and then back out the window.

Sarah didn't answer.

Tindra shouted, "Hey, there's Mrs. Lee!"

A red vehicle drove by slowly. Sure enough, Mrs. Lee sat

in the front, her shoulder-length blond hair under a black hat. She was slowing down by the gallery.

"I wonder where she is going," Leif said.

Tindra watched the car pull over in front of the gallery. "She lives close to the dock. She's an excellent artist. In the summer she takes over the gallery while our family goes on holiday to Italy." Tindra smiled.

"Wait a minute. Look! She just stopped and let the guy in her car!" Sarah observed.

"They obviously know each other," Leif commented.

"Excuse me." An elderly man was trying to exit the café.

"Oh, sorry." Sarah quickly opened the door for the man, while looking wide-eyed at Tindra. "This is the weirdest thing ever."

"Well, it's not that weird. Maybe he's a friend or relative of Mrs. Lee. Some sort of visitor," Tindra brainstormed.

"Yeah, a visitor that told me some pretty weird stuff!" Sarah said.

"What kind of weird stuff? He's probably just some obnoxious guy trying to hit on you." Tindra eyed the café counter hoping to direct Sarah's attention that way.

"Yeah, you're right." Sarah agreed.

Sarah finally followed Tindra back to the counter. Leif lingered at the entrance, watching out the window, before joining them. They all took a moment to order their drinks and pay at the counter, and then continued to walk through the town with their steaming hot chocolates in hand.

"What did he say, Sarah?" Leif asked.

Sarah continued her story, surprised that he wanted to know. "He was talking about how I was the one, the next in line…" Sarah stopped, not sure if she wanted to repeat the nonsense that he'd told her. She supposed that it really didn't matter, it was all completely crazy, but there was something within Sarah that made her wonder about him—and more so about this entire town and why she was seeing strange stuff.

"To do what?" Leif asked. She looked at him and then at Tindra. She wrapped her hands around the hot chocolate.

"To …" She hesitated. "To restore the Painter's Keep. Something like that. Like, what does that even mean?" She laughed nervously, feeling somewhat courageous in sharing it with her friends.

"Weird," Tindra commented mid-sip.

Leif didn't respond. He took a sip of his drink.

"He was telling me to be careful and stuff like that." Sarah shared. They all walked without speaking for a few seconds.

"Sounds like he's looking for someone important, in whatever world he's living in," Tindra laughed. "But 'Painter's Keep', I've heard that before."

"What, really?" Sarah asked, surprise dancing in her eyes. Leif looked surprised too.

"It's in a book that my mom used to read to me as a kid. It's one of my favorites. I'll have to show it to you," Tindra said casually. "It's like a fairy tale, I guess, but this one is kind of underground. At least, that's what my mom says."

"It would be cool to see that," Sarah replied, secretly wanting to run over to Tindra's house to see the book right at that moment. She asked, "What do you mean by underground? Like, for the story you were talking about."

"Just not popular, not mainstream. I mean, you can find the book if you are really set on finding it, I'm sure," Tindra shared. "It's called *Adventures Within the Startrail*."

Sarah looked up at Leif who seemed very deep in thought. He wasn't the only one. The word "Startrail" hit her head like a gong, as if there was a big orchestra about to sound off in her mind. It was a word that sounded familiar, but she couldn't understand why. Sarah pondered why a grown man would be mentioning something that was in a fairy tale.

"OK, so you've seen the café, the gallery is across the street, and the library is right here." Tindra raised her arm towards the left where it stood. "The library is only cool because of the tower. It's high up and it overlooks the town. Sometimes kids will hang out there late at night because there's nowhere else to go. There are stairs in the back to get to the top."

She pointed to the beautiful library tower. It had an old-world look to it and there was a bell snuggled right into the peak. They wandered up to the top and looked out. You could see all of Walton. As small as it was, it had its charm; the little shops added character. The ocean was like a blue blanket, lining the town shore and the late afternoon light glazed over the ocean surface. A lighthouse could be seen further out, past the town limits and suburban neighborhoods. Sarah enjoyed the view and looked back at Leif, who was looking directly at her. He had a serious look on his face. Tindra was at the other side of the tower looking over the edge.

"Sarah—I need to tell you something," he whispered. "About that guy."

"OK. Tell me. Why the whisper?"

"I just can't say right now. But it's important."

Tindra whirled around and walked back toward Leif and Sarah. "What are you talking about?"

"Oh, nothing." Leif said quickly.

"That's cool that Mrs. Lee is an artist," Sarah said as they walked back down the steps.

"Yeah, she is seriously so talented. We all moved out here together ten years ago from Stavanger," Tindra shared.

"Stavanger? Norway?" Leif questioned, looking at Tindra with surprised eyes. "That is where I am from!"

"I knew you were from Norway, but I didn't know which city," Tindra said. "What a coincidence!"

"Wait, so you're both from Norway." Sarah stopped abruptly.

Tindra smiled. "I guess it's kind of strange." She turned toward Leif. "Although, you just got here and I came here, like, over a decade ago. I was only seven when we moved."

Sarah was deep in her thoughts.

"There must be something special about Walton to bring you all here," she reflected while looking around. Maybe Gale was right, that Walton had something unique about it. Leif was quiet for a while as they walked back onto the street. He looked into Sarah's eyes while Tindra was talking about some festival that took place in the town. Whatever it was that Leif was trying to tell Sarah was going to have to wait.

CHAPTER 11

The three of them made their way toward the gallery and stopped on the sidewalk in front of it; it was within an old Victorian-style home with a wrap-around patio. It was very quaint. The windows showcased pieces of artwork on easels, and a sign with information about art lessons was stuck to the glass. Tindra opened the creaking old-fashioned door and it chimed as it closed behind them.

Leif grabbed Sarah by the hand. "Wait." She turned toward him. "I think we should go."

"What are you talking about?" Sarah looked at him strangely. "We just got here."

"The guy that you said told you that stuff—" Leif paused, looking nervous. "He is after something. I think I may know who he is."

"What is he after?" Sarah said. "Leif, you're scaring me."

"No, no, I'm sorry. Listen, whatever you have with you in your pocket. It is valuable."

"Guys, come on!" Tindra opened the door to Leif and Sarah, interrupting their conversation.

Sarah gasped, her eyes widening at all the beautiful paintings everywhere. There were landscapes and portrayals of the ocean and sailboats. Blues, turquoise, and greens jumped off the walls. Sarah's heart felt like it was floating, she almost forgot what Leif was trying to tell her. There was one painting especially that stood out to her. It had a sparkling yellow field and the bluest skies one could imagine. It felt like Sarah could walk right into it. She could almost feel the breeze in the air, within the painting. Entranced, Sarah stopped in front of it and examined the detail. It looked so real. The colors almost oozed out of the canvas, piercing her eyes with radiance.

A smiling woman approached them, pulling Sarah out of the moment.

The sheen on her purple dress caught the light. Her hair was neatly braided into a bun. Tindra hugged the woman, who Sarah assumed to be her mother. "How was school today?"

"Oh, boring as usual." Tindra yawned.

Leif lingered by the doorway; Sarah noticed he was looking antsy.

"Boring? This world is full of beauty that people don't take the time to see!" Tindra's mother said. "If I had it my way, schools would be all about painting, art, and expression. I see you have some friends here today!" She looked towards Sarah and cast a suspicious glance at Leif. "Welcome to the Walton Art Gallery. I'm Mrs. Valerie, Tindra's mom."

Sarah was about to reply, but Mrs. Valerie continued.

"Actually, call me Aura. Why all the formalities?" she said, full of energy.

"Nice meeting you," Sarah said with a smile. Tindra's mom was warm, kind and full of life. Sarah immediately felt refreshed, it made her glad that she'd stopped by the gallery.

"Mom, this is Sarah, she's new at our school," Tindra

informed her. Aura Valerie nodded and smiled as she looked at Sarah. "And this is Leif, he's also new. And he just moved here from Norway. Just like us, ten years ago."

"Hi there, Leif. Is that so?" Aura's voice faltered. "What brought you and your family out this way?"

"My father's work." He smiled. Sarah noticed that Leif looked nervous while talking to Mrs. Valerie.

"Oh, well, that's nice," Aura replied. "Oh, Tindra, I forgot to tell you that Mrs. Lee will be coming over for supper later. Her friend is in town and he wants to meet us." Aura glanced at Sarah before turning towards Tindra.

Sarah could detect a slight accent in Mrs. Valerie's voice. She now knew the type of accent it was. Norwegian. She turned back toward the painting of the yellow fields. It looked as though the sky was as blue as an ocean. As Tindra and Aura spoke, Sarah wandered closer to the painting. There was something so serene about it, something calming and familiar. It was almost overwhelming, and she couldn't look away. Minutes seemed to fly by, and her eyes were getting foggy. Realizing that her eyes were filled with tears, she brought her sleeves up to wipe them.

Leif looked over at her. "You are moved by this one."

Tindra wandered up to her and looked back at her mom who was also noticing Sarah's reaction to the painting.

Sarah was startled, "I don't know what came over me. What is this painting of? Like, is it a real place?"

"Art has a way of doing that to people," Tindra's mom smiled. "It has the power to stir emotion. This one is of a real place." She paused and looked at Leif. Leif was awkward again and looked down. "It's nowhere near here, of course."

"It's so familiar though," Sarah said. "I'm certain I've been there. Is it in Maine?"

"Maybe you've been somewhere like it, dear, but this

place is really far away," Aura said carefully. Leif watched Mrs. Valerie as she spoke about the painting.

Tindra changed the subject. "Mom, do you think we could do some painting today?"

Sarah's eyes lit up and she looked at Aura Valerie and back at Leif. Leif smiled at her.

"Well, sure, we have a couple of hours before dinner. I don't see why not," Aura reasoned.

Forgetting that she should check in with Gale, Sarah agreed to do the painting.

Aura Valerie went to get the materials to set them up.

Sarah continued to wander around the gallery. Leif stayed by the entrance.

"It's as if there's a whole world in each painting," Sarah said, full of conviction.

"Yes, well, you have said a true statement." Aura Valerie looked over at Leif as she opened a cabinet full of oil paintings.

"Oh yeah, like you could walk right into the painting!" Tindra's eyes lit up. "Oh, Mom, that's exactly like that old book! The paintings that are living. That you can go into."

Sarah immediately flashed back to the strange painting in her house that she swore her finger went through.

Tindra continued, "I told Sarah about the fairy tale book that you used to read to me? You know, the one about the Painter's Keep, and the portals that they paint to get from realm to realm, and the Startrail?" Tindra spoke casually as she fiddled with her phone.

Leif finally spoke up. "Where did your family get that book, Tindra?"

There was a crash as Aura Valerie suddenly dropped a framed painting she'd been holding and the glass broke on the floor. "Oh, whoops."

Tindra rushed to help her pick it up.

"I am sorry about that. Silly me. Yes, that little book. We haven't looked at that in years," Aura Valerie quickly said, while looking up at Sarah as if to say something more. Deciding against it, she resumed cleaning up the broken frame. Shattered glass was everywhere.

"Sarah said some weird guy asked her about the Painter's Keep. I didn't think anyone else knew about that book!" Tindra laughed and looked at Sarah. Sarah felt embarrassed by the attention, and by all of the confusion that went along with what seemed to be a silly story.

"Is that right?" Aura Valerie said. She stopped sweeping up the broken glass and looked at Sarah. "Where did you see him? Did you happen to see him with Mrs. Lee?"

"Yeah, we saw them together. He just kept overloading me with information," Sarah shared.

"What kind of information?" Aura asked, genuinely interested. Her face took on a serious expression. Leif stood next to her, equally serious.

"Just weird stuff. It's just all too strange." She felt embarrassed to share any more of what he had said to her, and yet there was a part of her that wanted to get it off her chest. The phone rang. Aura just stood with the broom, deep in thought. It rang a couple more times.

"Mom, do you want me to get it?" Tindra finally asked.

"No, no, I've got it. What has gotten into me?" Aura laughed nervously and zipped over to where the phone was in a back office.

The skies were beginning to grow darker; Sarah could see it from the windows. It was like a shadow suddenly came over the gallery. A grumbling of thunder followed. Sarah wandered the shop while Tindra went to find them some snacks from the back. Aura Valerie swiftly returned from the phone call and finished setting up the canvases and their painting stations near the back of the gallery. "This is where I hold most of my classes. Sarah, you should take one some-time. Tindra joins on occasion!"

Sarah nodded. "I'd love that."

Aura looked at Leif. "You are welcome too, Leif."

Leif smiled at Aura. "Thanks."

Aura looked at Leif carefully. "Who did you say your father was?"

Leif was texting on his phone and tried not to look up, it was like he didn't want to answer her. "Oh yeah, I didn't mention that."

Tindra jumped in. "He's from the same place as us—Stavanger." Leif looked relieved.

"Interesting," Aura replied.

Aura Valerie placed some brushes on the table next to the oil paints. "Where is it that you are from, Sarah?"

"Maine. From Augusta, Maine," Sarah said.

"Maine. There's a lot of magic in Maine, just like here," Aura replied while setting out the various colors of paint for them to use.

Tindra started sharing more about her day at school and the various assignments that she'd been given in her classes.

Sarah reflected on seeing the eye in the leaf, the keys, and the sparkles in the trees. She pressed her hand against her head, she felt a headache coming on.

Tindra looked at her as she sat on her stool in front of the canvas. "Are you OK?"

"Yeah." Sarah closed her eyes and opened them, deter-mined to ward the migraine off. She didn't want the atten-tion on her. "It's like certain things make the migraines start up and I don't know why."

"Like what?"

"It's hard to explain. Just, like, talking about all the weird stuff that happened today, it makes it come back."

She focused on the painting. Leif decided not to paint and

sat on a stool by the easels. The stations were set up, Sarah and Tindra committed to some colors of choice and started dabbing paint on the canvas. The dabs became smooth lines of dark blues and light blues. Sarah felt at ease as she made bigger strokes with the paintbrush; the joy of painting was coming back to her.

Ever since her dad went to jail, it was as if something or someone was trying to tell her something. Or as if her past, her memories from before, were trying to break their way through. She almost felt as if they were flowing through the paintbrush, onto the canvas.

How could that even ever matter now? She told herself. What mattered was to move on from the accident and make do. And now, finding strange keys that followed her. Was life really that supernatural? What was she supposed to do with it all?

Sarah paused to look at Leif. She noticed that he was watching her carefully, focusing on the pocket that had the keys. She felt the keys, they were warming up. Her heart started racing; she didn't want them to start floating or doing anything weird. She wished that Leif had told her what he knew, but it would have to wait.

A blast of thunder pounded over the gallery.

"Wow—rain's coming," Aura commented.

Just then, Sarah felt a surge within herself. A surge coming from deep inside. It was streaming down her arms and into her hands. The paintbrush in her hand felt like glass, like it would shatter with her strength. Her hand felt shaky as she moved the brush towards the canvas.

Just as she touched the canvas with the paintbrush, she became aware of the keys in her pocket and the vision of the vase pouring out some sort of liquid. The hand held out the keys and the eye in the leaf was watching. The paint made a mark on the canvas, but Sarah shot back. It was as if there was some sort of power coming out of the brush, like an electric shock. It forced her backwards and she fell onto the ground.

Tindra dropped her paintbrush and rushed over to Sarah. "Are you OK?"

Aura ran over too, and helped Sarah up.

"I'm fine. But … I dunno what just happened."

They all looked over at the canvas. The mark she had made with the paint was there, it was a single splotch in the middle of the canvas. But it wasn't the color that she had on the brush. Instead it was a gold color.

"I couldn't seem to do what I wanted to do. There was a power that overtook me." Sarah was standing there. The paintbrush had broken in two. One piece was on the ground and the other was in her hand, the brush part still attached. "I'm so sorry. I … I shouldn't have come here."

No one said anything for what seemed to be minutes. Sarah slowly looked around, spinning the broken brush in her hand, trying to make sense of it all.

Leif was wide-eyed as he helped her out. "This is what I was trying to tell you. Sarah, what's in your pocket … The power that you have …" He then looked up at Aura with a critical eye. "Don't tell me you don't know what's going on here."

Tindra was standing there, dumbfounded. "What is going on here?" She looked at her mother and then back at Leif.

"Something strange is happening to me and no one can understand, no one will ever get it." Sarah let the words pour out. "Why would Tindra's mom know what is going on, Leif? No one does. Honestly. I could try to explain, but you …" She paused; the tears were beginning to start. "Like everyone else, you wouldn't get it."

"We can try, Sarah," Tindra quickly said.

Leif walked toward her. "Sarah. Let's get you out of here."

She glanced over at Tindra's canvas, it was a painting of a tulip. It was nice, simple and bright. She noticed other unfinished paintings leaning against the wall or up on the counters in the work area. Then there was hers. A big, blotchy mess of a painting. Undefined, unnecessary, confusing. Just like her life.

"You may be trying to uncover a gift, Sarah," Aura said almost in a whisper. But Sarah was halfway out the door. Sarah could tell she wanted to help, but she was confused. She started walking in the pouring rain in the direction of Gale's house, her hand still clinging to the broken paint brush. She was about to throw it into the bushes but reached into the side pocket of her bag and placed it there instead.

"Sarah, wait!" Leif called out to her as he followed her outside.

"What just happened in the gallery, Leif?" She felt angry. "I'm a freak. I make no sense."

He stood at a distance. "I was trying to tell you."

"Tell me what? Nothing you can say will be what I need to hear," Sarah shouted. "My whole life is a crazy, boring mess, filled with all sorts of confusion because of an accident that messed everything up. My mom left us. My dad's confused. I have no answers, you have no answers."

She was about to take out the keys and show them to Leif but stopped herself. She put her hands in the pocket of her jacket and felt the keys. This time they weren't warm, they were almost hot. She thought about the vision she had about the vase and the voice saying to *put the keys together* and then thought about the strange man who told her to *be careful,* and said that she was the *one* that *they* were waiting for. Her mind was playing tricks on her again, that had to be what was happening. Either there was something more to the story and there was a reason for all her findings, or she was just going crazy. Maybe she needed to be with her dad, locked away—locked away from the madness.

There's more, there's more. Those words that her dad told her, what did it all mean?

"Sarah!" Mrs. Valerie shouted out from the gallery patio. Tindra stood behind her, sheltered under the patio roof.

"There's nothing more to say," Sarah said to them. Leif stepped forward toward her. "Leave me alone. I'm sorry, I just need to figure this out on my own."

Leif turned to look at Aura before turning away.

Leif stepped down the patio stairs and started walking down the street.

"Wait, Leif. Tell me what you know!" Sarah heard Aura ask.

Sarah turned to look back, Leif was turned toward Aura for a moment but she couldn't make out the words that he said.

CHAPTER 12

Sarah ran up to her room, drenched from the rain, and fell on her bed. The storm had ended by the time she reached Gale's house. The liquid moonlight seemed to mirror her teary eyes. She lifted her arms; they were still shaking subtly from the power that shot through her at the gallery. Did she have some sort of powers? An ability that she was just becoming aware of? Maybe she should run away, back to Augusta, stay with Stina and her family, and just try and sort it all out. Or maybe run away from everyone, forever.

The vision of the vase, the liquid, and the word "Startrail" popped into her mind.

She took out her phone and decided to look up the word.

She put it in search but there was nothing she could find that was relevant. She looked for another few minutes. Just as she was about to put her phone down, she saw it.

Startrail: Earth Realm: Walton - Annie Holt. 9 Port Street

Walton. Walton? She sat up on her bed.

It was 8:00 p.m. She walked downstairs, the keys warm in her pocket.

"Gale?"

There was no reply; the house was empty, Gale's office was empty. She grabbed some juice, sat down at the table, and searched "Startrail" once again. Nothing new came up other than the address in Walton.

She received a message from Tindra.

Tindra: Are you back home?

Sarah answered. She felt bad for leaving so suddenly, but she felt embarrassed about what had happened.

Sarah: Yeah. I'm so sorry about what happened.

Tindra: Don't even worry about it. Whatever happened was just a silly accident.

Sarah: This might seem really weird but do you think I could see that Startrail book of yours? You know - the one you said your mom read to you as a kid?

Tindra: I'll bring it tomorrow. What do you want it for?

She didn't respond.

Gale was still out. It had stopped raining hard and began to drizzle again. Sarah decided to take a walk over to the address that had come up with the Startrail reference. She told herself that this would be her last step to finding out what was going on. If she didn't find anything, she would throw the keys into the ocean and let it go forever. That is, if the keys stayed away.

She put on her jacket and a beanie and used Google Maps to direct her. It wasn't very far, just past the gallery and up the next street. Port Street.

The wind was picking up and blew her hat off. She ran after it up the street and retrieved it. Eventually she stood in front of a little blue bungalow. Nine Port Street. The lights were on, like all of the other houses in the street. All the events that had led up to this moment flooded her memory. She was driven to find an answer, and now there was someone who could help her understand what the

Startrail really was. She braced herself to knock on the door.

There was no answer. She was about to turn away when the door suddenly opened. She held the address that she had written down in her hand. In her surprise, the sheet of paper dropped out of her hand, falling to the ground.

"Sarah?"

"Mrs. Valerie?" Sarah was backing toward the sidewalk now. "I'm sorry, I …"

"Are you looking for Tindra?" Mrs. Valerie picked up the sheet of paper that had fallen.

"No, never mind. I've got to go."

She looked at the paper. "You are looking for Annie, I see."

"Got the wrong house." Sarah took off down the street.

"Sarah, wait!"

Sarah shivered in her jacket and ran. Stars were sparkling in the now clear evening sky; the slice of moon watched her run. She felt that she had made things worse. Now they must really think she's crazy.

Tindra was running down the street after her. She was just turning past the gallery.

"Sarah, what are you doing?!" Tindra yelled. "My mom said you came to the house."

"Yeah, wrong address," she kept walking.

"Well, what house were you looking for?"

The winds continued to pick up, almost knocking them over.

She felt the keys move in her pocket. "I was looking for nine Port Street."

"That's my house." Tindra hesitated. "Well, who were you looking for?"

"Do you know Annie Holt?"

"Annie Holt?" Tindra paused. "Uh, nope, I don't think so."

"Annie Holt is attached to your address," Sarah said. "I looked up Startrail online and there was this one thing that I found, the only relevant thing. Your address, and the name Annie Holt."

"What? That's so weird. Do you still have it on your phone?"

Sarah showed it to her.

"I've never heard of her. I mean, the Startrail book is all I know about the Startrail ... maybe the name has to do with the book."

Just then, someone stepped out from behind a tree, blocking their way.

They both leaped back.

"Whoa, watch it!" Tindra said.

It was a man wearing dark clothes and a black winter jacket. He had thick black hair and his eyes were black. He didn't budge. When they tried to walk around him, he moved with them. He was very tall, taller than any human that Sarah had ever seen.

"Leave us alone!" Sarah shouted.

"I'm not here to hurt you," the man said calmly. He looked around as if there were others watching him. "I'm here to help you."

"What are you talking about?" Sarah said.

"Time is of the essence, so please tell me. If you have come across any of the keys, you need to come with me, right now, or hand it over. Orders of Panveer," the man continued. He looked back a couple times and Sarah noticed that he squeezed his fist.

"Keys?" Tindra questioned, looking at Sarah slightly. She obviously remembered the key that Sarah had found. "You must have us mistaken for someone else."

"Your friend knows very well." His black eyes stared right into Sarah's eyes. Sarah felt weak, like he was physically making her lose power. She tried to look away, trying to maintain herself, to regain control, but she couldn't help but feel lightheaded.

"Sarah, what is he talking about? He can't be talking about that key you found?" She looked at Sarah, wide-eyed, waiting for answers. They began to back away towards the gallery.

Sarah saw Tindra pulling out her phone. She was grateful. She couldn't even do that; her strength was being zapped from her.

"We can detect that you have been amongst the stardust that is in this region. It's within you. We have been sent out to every realm, to all the stardust pockets where the keys may have been sent." The man walked closer towards her. "Panveer would rather see you in person, so come with me. If you won't come with me, do the smart thing and hand them over. You'll be glad you did."

Tindra had the phone in her hand. She was trying to grapple with sending for help while keeping away from the strange man. She tried to run, but before she could take a step, he grabbed her arm. The leaves crunched below his feet and a gust of cold wind waved through the man's hair, revealing its length down his back. As he gripped Tindra's arm, she dropped her phone. Sarah could see that it was calling someone. Never had she felt so weak. It was as if she had just run a marathon, but all within a couple of minutes of time.

"Let me go! Help!" Tindra shouted.

"I guess your friend will do." He still had Tindra by the arm, and began to lift her off the ground as she struggled. "Do your friend a favor and tell me where the key is. This can all be done very, very peacefully. We actually are here to help you."

"Let her go!" The words were a struggle, too. She tried to

lift her head and it felt like a weight. She fell sideways onto the ground. "Let her go!"

The man laughed. "Is that what you have amounted to? What a joke. Panveer is in for a disappointment. Why the keys would come to someone as weak as you is beyond me."

Another man emerged from the trees behind the gallery. "If she doesn't have it with her, leave it." He was small compared to the long-haired man. He looked at Sarah with careful eyes. "You are Silver, aren't you?"

"No. My name is Sarah." Sarah managed to say, still weak and crouching on the ground.

"All the *Esmerelda Letters* say is that it is Silver who will be the next Keeper. Not Sarah," the other man said quickly. He looked as though he didn't want to get involved. "It's Silver of Ocean Sky we want. So, let's get going."

"She's not of Earth Realm. Tell me I'm not the only one who can see that."

"Yes, I see that. But this realm is finicky. The starpools and areas with ample stardust will make for situations like this. Let's go, Reo." the smaller man said. "Although, it is interesting how much she holds. Or is it what she holds?"

They saw someone running down the street towards them. It was Tindra's father.

"Hey!" he shouted, pointing at the tall man. "Let them go!"

Other voices could be heard beyond him.

"Drop her!" Fathom Valerie stood in front of the tall man who laughed in his face.

The other man continued to be more reasonable. "Drop the girl, Reo."

The tall man reluctantly complied.

"Run to the house, Tindra. Take Sarah with you," Fathom said.

"But Dad, Sarah just collapsed, she can't get up," Tindra

replied, tears in her eyes as she rubbed her arm. Sarah tried to stand.

"How dare you enter this realm and make the claims that you do?" Fathom looked briefly at Tindra before facing Reo. "Leave now. Tell Panveer that he is confused. No keys have been found. You should leave this realm. You're not accustomed to the lack of stardust here." He said the last part with grit in his voice. Tindra was looking at her father like he was speaking a new and foreign language.

"We know that she has the key. We have been given instructions to find Silver of Ocean Sky. We must take her with us, and the key, as Panveer has ordered. You would do well to abide by those orders too. Unless, of course, you want me to inform him that there is a colony living here in this realm that has been forgotten about for years." The man spat as he talked. He looked around. "This world is drab anyway. Don't know how you people stand it."

"You're going to want to be careful what you say," Fathom said sharply. Sarah watched in awe of Tindra's dad's confidence and fearlessness.

"Or what? Your powers don't work here, friend. The air tastes stale. There's not enough stardust." He stuck out his tongue and brought it back in to savor. "The power we have brought with us will be enough to overpower you. Therefore, you ought to change your mindset." He spat again. "You know, see the truth."

"I wouldn't be so sure," Tindra's dad said quietly.

"It's no wonder the evacuation is happening soon. This place is done for."

"Evacuation?" Fathom asked.

"The keys are missing. No seafaen. No portals. No realms," Reo continued. "You know what? Take them, we need to go."

Fathom stepped back and braced himself. "Don't you even try."

"What are you going to do? There are no Portal Painters who have any power, here, or anywhere, now that the Painter's Keep isn't accessible. Panveer's plan B is your only hope."

The man moved menacingly toward Fathom. Fathom put his arm straight out. Did he believe that he would stop him just with his hand? The man grabbed him by the throat and threw him down.

"Dad!" Tindra shouted and ran over to him. Sarah was still trying to regain her footing.

"Go to the house, Tindra," Fathom said as he struggled to get back up.

"Your powers are lacking here, Fathom," Reo said. "What's it to you that the girl comes with us? Why do you care?"

As he grabbed Fathom again, Aura appeared with something shining in her hand. To Sarah's surprise, it looked like a bright diamond the size of an apple. Aura lifted the diamond forward towards Reo as he was about to lift Fathom up again, and he flew backwards and hit a tree. The shorter man ran toward Aura, but the diamond created a force that pushed him back too. He got back up and made a move toward Sarah, but Fathom regained his strength and raised his fist towards the man's face. Sarah noticed that his eyes suddenly flashed to black.

"Tough guy now."

Aura walked down toward them, holding the diamond in front of her. "Stay away. You say there's no stardust here. Maybe you're all wrong. Leave Sarah alone and go."

"Panveer will know what you did here, and you and your little settlement of Erleonians will need to answer to him," the man shouted. He brushed some dirt off his pants and went over to Reo, who had hit the tree.

Aura ran over to her husband. Fathom was standing again. "You are after the wrong person," he said. "Get out of here!"

"There is nothing here, so it's time for you two to leave this realm," Aura added.

They looked at Sarah who was now walking weakly with Mrs. Lee who had also come out to help. She and Tindra rushed her as fast as they could to the house. Fathom and Aura followed behind, ensuring that the strange men were gone.

Once they were all safely in the house. Fathom locked the door and closed the curtains. Sarah could tell that Tindra was confused. She had just heard her parents talk about so many strange things and do crazy things too.

Aura led Sarah over to one of the sofas. "Sit down here. Are you feeling better? Tindra, can you please get Sarah some water?"

"I still feel kind of dizzy." Sarah received the water from Tindra and drank it slowly while closing her eyes. "It was like he was sucking energy out of me. I felt so tired. His eyes were black!"

Aura nodded knowingly. "Yes, it's OK. That feeling will fade soon. Next time, don't look the agents right in the eye. You aren't used to … This is going to sound strange, but you aren't used to the exchanging of stardust and how it can be used to gain power."

Sarah tried to look at Aura but had to keep her eyes closed. She stayed seated on the sofa, trying not to move. What was she talking about?

"Aura, maybe don't tell them all about that just yet," Fathom said while pacing the living room floor, and continually peeking through the closed curtains to look out the window.

"Honey, it's not going to be hard for them to find us," Aura said casually. "We might as well explain everything."

She searched for Tindra, who was sitting on a dining room chair. "Is your arm OK, Tindra?"

"I don't care about my arm." Her voice was shaky and there were tears in her eyes. "What just happened out there?" Tindra was in shock, her eyes were glazed over, and she wouldn't look directly at anyone. "Dad, you were talking about realms and … and then, Mom, you came out and had this strange power that came out of that … that thing! Or was it out of you?"

Fathom and Aura looked like they didn't know how to address Tindra's questions.

"I'm sorry, Tindra. We will … we will explain it all. I promise. I didn't want this all to be exposed to you in this way," Fathom said.

Everyone stared at Sarah, like they had so much to ask and explain, and yet no one was explaining anything. It was like they were worried about saying the wrong thing.

"I have been seeing things." Sarah felt exposed and embarrassed. "I have so many questions. I came here thinking that someone named Annie Holt could help me."

Aura cleared her throat. "Annie Holt. Yes. Annie Holt would be me."

"You?" Sarah said.

"Mom, what are you talking about?"

"Annie Holt. It's just a …" Her voice faltered. "It's hard to explain. It's a fake name used to protect my true identity. This address is out there if anyone, like you, was needing to find us."

"I needed to find out more about the Startrail. I don't know why … I don't know why it keeps showing up, the word. People keep saying it to me or I dream about it."

Fathom turned and looked toward her. "Do you have any

idea about the Startrail? Does that ring a bell? Or the name Panveer?"

Aura shot a look at him with wide eyes. "What he's trying to say is, there are a lot of things out there that will be very new to you." She looked over and gave a sensitive smile to Sarah and Tindra. "Tindra why don't you go get the … the book that we were talking about before."

"What, why!?" Confusion was turning into anger; it was written all over Tindra's face. "Why aren't we calling the police, Dad? Instead, you want me to grab some kids' book?" She looked around. "And why isn't anyone explaining to me what is going on?"

Fathom and Aura looked at each other. Sarah could tell that they were trying to think of the right thing to say.

"Honey," Fathom called out to his daughter. He watched her storm up the stairs, his hands up in the air like he was going to say something else.

"*Startrail*," Mrs. Lee probed again. "You have no recollection of that word?"

Fathom looked upset that they continued to talk about it.

It felt like she was in a dream, within a scene that was so unfamiliar. Sarah's head panged. And then the word … the word Startrail was a jackhammer trying to drill at her brain. They had just been attacked by two strange men with powers that were unheard of, and Aura seemed to have power too. No one was calling the police. It was strange, but Sarah was immune to strange things.

Sarah rubbed her head. "Every time I hear that word, my head hurts so much. I only heard of it for the first time from Tindra, she said that she had this book about it or something." Sarah leaned forward. "I didn't know what he meant then, and I don't know what it means now." She leaned back against the couch and closed her eyes. "Then, there was this weird guy that told me all this stuff. It's just, it's too confusing."

Aura nodded towards Mrs. Lee as if she knew who the guy was. "She means Ivo. He walked right up to her, and—"

"Yes, he told me," Mrs. Lee confirmed. She shook her head. "I told him to be careful with what he said to people out here, but … I suppose we are all a little unsure how to deal with this. I told him that if he has any thoughts about someone being the Keeper, this Silver, to proceed with caution and not jump to conclusions. The average human would never understand any of this at this point."

"We know you're not Silver," Fathom said, "but …"

Sarah interrupted. She felt like her mind would burst. If everyone was sharing things, she might as well too. "I found two strange keys and they keep following me around. All the while, I can't help but feel that I am the wrong person. I mean, I have no idea about this … this …" She looked around at each person. "Startrail."

There was a long silence, a silence that felt heavy.

"Sarah. You found two keys?" Aura gasped and put her hand over her mouth, in awe of what she had just heard. She looked at Fathom.

"The keys are important. You must keep them safe," Mrs. Lee couldn't help but say. "I think we are just a little unsure why the keys came to you if you have no recollection of the Startrail. If we could see them, maybe we could help. It must mean something that you came across them."

"That's what I am saying. I'm not this Silver. I have no idea who that is," Sarah continued. "Why didn't any of you say anything to me before about any of this?"

"Sarah, we know that this area is full of hidden stardust and starpools, which is why we all chose to live here when we left after the war," Mrs. Lee said. "Never would we expect this to be the place where—" She stopped talking.

"I think this is too much right now," Aura said quickly.

Sarah was taken aback; all eyes were on her. She looked toward the stairs and Tindra was slowly walking back down. She sat across from Sarah.

Aura walked up to Tindra and Fathom pressed on. "If you found them, then that means you are …" He looked at Mrs. Lee, Tindra and Aura, then back at Sarah. "Then you would be the Keeper of the Painter's Keep. But …"

"And a Portal Painter," Aura said in a whisper. They all looked at her solemnly. "The power that came out of you at the gallery …"

Tindra was watching in confusion.

"No, I'm nothing, it's nothing," Sarah said abruptly. She was feeling more energized from just sitting down for a while, but her familiar headache had started again. It was the word Startrail and all this confusing talk that brought it back. At least, that was what caused it before. She continued softly, "Listen, it means nothing. It's all just random. I don't have anything to do with this stuff. My dad, he's in jail." Tears started behind her eyes. She paused and looked down at her hands, and then looked up again. Everyone was still listening. Some looked away, but others still watched. "I don't even know where my mother is, she left us when I was young. And, I don't have memories like everyone else. Maybe it's from the car accident that my dad and I were in ten years ago. Or maybe it's because there is nothing to remember." Sarah swallowed and breathed deeply. "I have to leave. I shouldn't have let my dad convince me to move here."

Everyone was quiet. Waiting and hesitant.

"You know what, we need to stop here. Sarah is being dragged into this without us knowing why the keys arrived here, anyway." Aura shrugged.

"Maybe we should see if they are even the keys that we

are hoping for," Fathom suggested. He watched Tindra who was now sitting next to Sarah on the couch.

"Those men out there are after the keys. Panveer obviously wants them back," Aura said. "And they know where we are."

"Only the right person finds the keys. This is how it works. The keys always know where they should go," Mrs. Lee persisted. She looked empathetic. "I am sorry, Sarah, but bear with us. I think that you need to reach deep down and try to think if you remember."

Sarah stood up abruptly. "I ... I don't know the Painter's Keep, I don't know the Startrail, I don't know what these keys are for, and I don't want anyone's help. I can't remember anything from before the accident. This is why your assignment on memories was hard for me."

"We all know that the keys have been sent out. This means that Panveer ..." Fathom paused and looked at Sarah, searching her face quickly. "The United Ones, since the war ten years ago, have been relying on having control of the keys. Keeping access only to themselves, allowing them to use the seafaen for themselves. The Keeper of the Keys was lost during the war, and the keys taken by Ashook. But now, the keys have been sent out, which means someone actively did this, in search of the new Keeper."

"Hope for the Painter's Keep." Aura held her hands together. Hope in her eyes. "Erleon is looking out for us."

"We need to talk to Mildred and Jack in Norway. The Painter's Keep was guarded by the Keeper, Esmerelda the Betrayer," Fathom added, "under the control and power of Ashook. Whether Esmerelda is alive anymore, we don't know. She must be, in order to access the Painter's Keep, unless there's another Keeper under his control. But we do know that Ashook had control of the keys, and now Panveer, his son. And we know that none of our Portal

Painters in hiding have been able to access the Painter's Keep."

"But once the three keys are put together by the new Keeper, then this can happen again. They can access and rebuild the Painter's Keep and the Startrail," Mrs. Lee beamed.

"This is urgent news," Fathom replied. "Go and call Mildred and we will find out. Sarah, you don't need to worry about anything. We'll find out what we can, and try to help you understand what you saw today and what you have been experiencing. And the same with you, Tindra." He sat on a chair in front of her. "Tindra, I am so sorry. There were reasons that we couldn't share this with you. We were all in hiding after the war."

Tindra looked up at her father. "Why didn't you tell me that you had powers?"

"I know it doesn't make sense. Please bear with us, we will explain everything, and maybe … maybe you'll remember some things about the place that we used to live in?" Aura continued.

Sarah breathed in deeply and exhaled; she stood up and turned to leave. All this strange talk was obviously not going to stop.

"Sarah, wait!" Aura stood up. "Forgive us, we are all a little unsure with how to proceed. There's a lot we need to share with you. There is a lot that just happened, and you can't go out there right now. Who knows where those men are?"

"Please tell us where the keys are," Fathom asked, arms crossed, a serious look on his face. "It's a good thing that they didn't end up in the wrong hands."

She shook her head, she felt unheard and confused. It was as if they forgot that she had never heard about any of this before.

"Is this all a joke?" She looked around hoping that

someone would crack a smile and say that it was all pretend, but deep down she knew that there needed to be a reason for all the strange stuff that was happening. The truth was that she had the keys with her. They were in her pocket, but she wished she was rid of them. Maybe she should hand them over and be done with it. But she knew that they would just come back to her. "As far as I know, I have just confirmed that I need to go back to Augusta."

Tindra walked to the door with her. "I really don't know what is going on. But I do know that this … this flimsy little book"—she looked through it before handing it to Sarah—"It will explain it to you, about the Startrail. It looks like I have been lied to ever since we moved here." She looked at her parents and then at the floor. "But …" She paused, thoughtfully. "I know that it was probably for a good reason. And if this is real, then it is a good reason."

She smiled, her chin wrinkled as she aimed to hold in tears. Aura put her arm around Tindra.

Sarah took the book reluctantly from her.

"Let me make this clear. I have no idea about anything you are talking about. To me, everything that I have experienced is one big mistake. It's random. It has nothing to do with me," Sarah said. She turned around and walked out the door.

"Let us walk with you," Fathom said. "We'll drive you home, Sarah. I don't know your Aunt Gale very well, but please be careful who you trust."

"Aunt Gale is the only family I have right now. Why wouldn't I trust her? My dad entrusted me to her. I just need to be alone right now." Sarah had never called Gale "Aunt Gale" until now. Deep down she wasn't sure if she trusted her either, but for now, she would stick up for her. Why would she trust Tindra's parents over her own flesh and blood?

The words *Protect the keys, you are the chosen one* came over her. Stop it! She tried to urge herself to stop thinking such strange things.

"I looked up Startrail and found Annie Holt. I came here to find out more, but this is beyond what I could imagine would happen. You know what? YOU guys take them." She pulled the two glimmering keys out of her pocket and dropped them onto the carpet in front of Fathom.

There was a silence in the room. They all stared in wonder. No one grabbed the keys.

Sarah turned and ran out the door into the cold night. She was relieved to be rid of the keys.

"We are here to help you!" Aura stepped forward and yelled out the door.

She needed to get away. The information felt like a crowd of people moving in on her, telling her all about who she was supposed to be, what she was supposed to be about.

CHAPTER 13

They were stupid keys that didn't mean anything, and if Tindra's family wanted them and were so obsessed with them, then they could have them. It didn't matter. Her jog turned into a fast walk. Sarah blinked hard. She saw something on the ground immediately in front of her. The keys were there, appearing as before, just like she knew they would. She bent over them and whispered, "I knew it." She kicked them away and kept walking, but they continued to follow her, appearing in front of her, like they were a part of her.

The evening sky was deep blue and clear. It looked like it was being held up by one bright star, like a pin. Sarah felt like the main street was the stage, the shops and sidewalk were the empty auditorium. The star was the spotlight, just watching her, waiting for her to do something exciting. Everyone was waiting for her to do something that mattered, but they had the wrong person, they had the wrong girl. What did they want her to do with these keys anyway? It made no sense. Her head pounded in pain. She closed her eyes and breathed in the autumn air, everything around her was so quiet. Just Sarah, alone with her thoughts. She stood in the stillness for a moment before continuing to walk.

"Sarah!" Fathom jogged up behind her. "I am not letting you walk home after what happened earlier. Let me give you a drive. You may not understand it now, but you will someday. The keys aren't meant for us. They disappeared as soon as you turned to leave. And look—there they are in front of you."

"Please. I don't know anything you are saying." Sarah looked at him, confusion filling her mind, and she could feel the headache getting worse. She was about to take off running again. Not that she feared him, but more that she was too mixed up—mixed up by all the information that had been thrown at her. Anything else would just muddy the waters even further. "I don't want them. I don't."

"You could keep ignoring them, or you could take them and be open to what it all means," he said, eyes locked on her. "I wish I understood why they are coming to you. We must find out who Silver is, and then the keys can go to her. OK? There's a huge reality that you need to understand. It's strange to hear that, but that's why we are being careful with how we explain."

"Is this some sort of cult?" Sarah's mind was going a hundred miles a minute. Fathom was talking nonsense. She picked up the keys and put them in her pocket. "I'll find a way to get rid of them. I … I will find a way."

"Get rid of them?" Fathom questioned. There was desperation in his voice. "Please don't do that. We need them. In fact, there's …"

A vehicle turned up the street. "Sarah."

Leif was driving.

"Sarah—do you need a ride?"

Sarah ran towards his car.

"Wait, Sarah. Sarah!" Fathom called out.

She got into the vehicle, relieved to be with Leif. She watched Fathom fade into the distance as they drove off. Leif was driving with an intensity she had never seen in him before. "Sarah. There's been some …" He paused. "Visitors in the town lately."

She thought of the two men that attacked Tindra and her earlier.

She felt the keys move, she opened her pocket and they were hovering slightly. She tried to ignore them.

"These guys came out of nowhere, they were making all these claims," she said. "They lifted Tindra right off the ground."

"Yeah, Sarah, there's some crazy stuff going on. I'll take you to your aunt's. It's too hard to explain. Those guys, they didn't know what they were doing," Leif said. "I'm sorry I didn't say anything before."

"Wait, you know them? I need to get out of here. I don't want anything to do with the Startrail, and these keys …"

"That's what I want to talk to you about." Leif looked at Sarah. ""You have them with you now, don't you?" He pulled the car over. Sarah could see Gale's house up the hill.

"Why are you stopping?" Sarah looked at him.

"You mentioned keys. If they are the ones that I think they are, then …" Leif trailed off, like the rest was obvious.

"Why does everyone care about the keys?" Sarah looked into his eyes. If she had to trust anyone, she thought it would be him. "I found one here and I found one in Maine."

Leif looked conflicted. "If you have the keys, I—"

"You what?" Sarah felt impatient. What was he not saying?

"That's what was glowing in your pocket at school." He paused. "Then, at the art gallery. That power." Leif stumbled on his words. "Power came out of you, Sarah."

"They hold some strange power, don't they? Tell me what

you know, Leif!" Sarah felt a desperation she had never experienced before.

He looked down at the steering wheel and she looked at her hands like they were foreign to her, remembering what she'd felt at the gallery. Sarah waited for him to answer and set her gaze out the window. There was a gazebo with lights on the roof that could be seen through the forest. She remembered seeing it in the daylight; her Aunt Gale's was just up a narrow trail behind it, and the trails she took to school were to the left.

"Well, if you're not going to tell me, then …" She felt on the brink of tears. "Then I need to leave." She stepped out of the car and stood for a few moments. Leif got out too, watching her. "I don't know what sort of power came out of me, but something is going on within me. Maybe it's because of the keys."

The sky was dark, but it was clear except for a few clouds whipping past the moon. The air was crisp, hinting of winter. It smelled like soggy fall leaves mixed with pine. She walked toward the gazebo, pulling her sweater around her. The gazebo was nestled in the woods, in front of a pond. It was simple, painted white, and had lights dragged along the top of it. The white lights glimmered softly in the dark, matching the sparkle of the stars. She stood in front of the pond and then walked into the gazebo.

Leif followed after her. "Sarah, stop. What happened at the gallery is significant. I was trying to tell you that the keys, if you have them, they are super powerful."

She shook her head as she looked into the pond. "Then, tell me what you know! Please. My arms … I still feel that surge of energy."

"People find it difficult telling you anything because no one has seen anyone like you in Earth Realm for years." He looked at her carefully.

"Earth Realm?" She searched his face. "Now you're talking like them, too."

He suddenly turned toward her and grabbed her hands, his brown eyes focused on hers and his face intense. He breathed deeply.

"I'm not at liberty to say anything else," Leif said. He ran one hand through his hair. "I will tell you this. Those keys hold power—they can do crazy stuff like make people fly or float on their own. And they've been missing." Sarah stared back at him blankly. "I couldn't tell you before. I didn't know you had them. Yet."

"What?" Sarah backed away, deep in thought, her eyes focused on the pond. She noticed it had a strange illumination to it. "All my life has been a series of crazy, strange occurrences. Just tell me where these keys come from."

The pond was as clear as crystal and it bounced into Sarah's eyes like a shock of light in the deep darkness of the night. Her hand grazed the keys that were in her pocket; they were strangely warm again.

"Your life has been that way because you're meant for more. It's like you've been hidden." She could tell that Leif was struggling to find the words. "It just means that you … you are special, Sarah." He gazed into her eyes, full of interest.

Sarah felt her heart melt but tried to stay focused. "What do you mean 'hidden'?"

They both leaned out over the ledge of the gazebo and she looked down at his hand, still holding hers.

"I should be sorry." He stared at her intently. "I just didn't expect you to be like this. You know …" He looked away. "Cool. Like someone that I enjoy being with. When we came here, it wasn't just for my dad's work." Leif struggled with his words again. "My dad's work, well, it … it involves the keys."

"OK, well, why did they come to me?" She pulled out the

keys. The rubies caught glimpses of the moon, winking at it subtly. She turned one of them around in her hands and, satisfied with her brief inspection, she passed it over to Leif. The other one was placed on the ledge of the gazebo.

"You're honestly telling me that you haven't seen these keys before. You don't know anything about them?"

"Why would I?" Sarah said, confused by his questioning. She flashed back to the vision of the hand holding out the keys. It was like someone was telling her what was to come. It made no sense, but it wasn't something she knew about, unless it was a memory. A memory from before trying to make its way through. Her arms felt heavy again. Her heart began to pound, but in a steady determined way, a strong way. It was how she'd felt at the gallery.

"Wait a minute," Leif said, his eyes locked on the keys. "Look. What is happening?"

The keys began to float out of his grasp; they hovered slightly in the night.

"The pond," Leif said slowly. "It's moving too."

"It's rising. The water, it's rising!" Sarah said. Her arms were raised toward the pond, they were stretched out and straining. "My arms are doing it. I'm somehow making this happen."

The water in the pond rose like an inverted whirlpool. It shot up like a fountain, but it wasn't spraying anywhere. "It feels like there's a force within it pulling me in!"

Leif looked at her arms raised up towards the pond, confused, but in awe.

"Sarah! Be careful. Bring your arms down!" he shouted.

"I'm trying." Her voice shook and her arms felt heavy.

Nothing else was happening. The two keys were still floating beside them and the mound of liquid was spinning like a tornado. A quiet sound of wind seemed to come from it. They stared at it, expecting something crazy to happen, like an explosion, or something to come out of it. Her arms were still straight ahead, but she was able to move them slightly downwards. "I feel like there's a magnet pulling me."

"Let's get out of here," Leif said.

Leif grabbed her arm; concern was in his eyes. "Sarah, seriously, be careful. There's a lot about this place that you don't understand."

"And you do?" Sarah said, frightened, yet mesmerized by the sight.

"I know more than you think. You've got to trust me," Leif said carefully.

She looked back at him. "There's something within me controlling this. I don't know how, but …"

She turned away from him and focused on the water, walking carefully toward the sparkling liquid tower. There was a sudden peace within her, a confidence, the same confidence that she'd felt when she painted at the gallery. The power—the strange power was there, she could sense it. She needed to touch the water. It was still spinning the same way, as if it were waiting for them to do something or say something. She could see down into the pond. It looked like it fell deeper and deeper, almost like a tunnel. A tunnel of water. She reached out and touched it. It felt like normal water and it didn't flinch or move. But something shifted, whether it was within her or within the water, and she could see again in her mind's eye.

Within her mind she could see flashing colors, lights, and the hand with the three keys being held out. The same hand from the vision she'd had before. The vase with the liquid within it appeared as well. There were fields of stars in her view and then there was someone who she couldn't quite see. It wasn't that her eyes were closed; she could see this within the walls of the water. Her head became blurry and the migraine began. Then she heard a voice. "Protect the keys. If you are seeing this, protect them. You have been chosen as the Keeper of the Keys."

"Who are you?" Sarah asked in a whisper.

"You have seen me looking through," the voice said. The voice sounded strained or as if the person speaking was in pain. Sarah felt like she was in a trance; she no longer felt strong enough to hold the inverted water.

She felt Leif pull on her shoulders and then grab her hand to pull her back. Whatever power was creating the phenomenon seemed to hold her in.

"Sarah, I'm trying to pull you back. It's pulling you in. Hang on!" Leif's voice was strained.

Sarah felt him pull, but the water was like a magnet and she stayed in one place. Her mesmerizing awe turned into a fearful urgency to get away from the pond. She tried to turn around, to move toward Leif, but the force was strong. "Help me!"

Leif was struggling to pull her away. Sarah felt her feet enter the cold water.

"Hang on, Sarah!" Leif strained to keep her from going deeper into the water. "Agh!" He fell back, letting go of her arm a bit, and she was pulled in further. The water was cool and latched onto Sarah. He grabbed her again, keeping her from being completely submerged. Her other hand grasped at the fall leaves covering the soil beside the pond.

Another arm reached in suddenly and grabbed Sarah. It was the strange man with long blond hair, the man who'd told her that she was the chosen one, and about the Painter's Keep.

Together, Leif and the strange man managed to pull her away from the water's grip. They pulled her out far enough to be safe, past the gazebo and past the trees. Sarah's clothes were soaked. The strange man had his arm toward the water and seemed to make it go back to the way it was before. Flattened, like a regular pond. There was no evidence of anything different.

Sarah was on the ground, looking at the pond in complete awe. The keys fell to the ground, Leif picked them up and stood up quickly to face the man.

"Someone's got to watch out for her," the other man said under his breath. "Doesn't look like you're doing a great job of it."

"You don't even know me," Leif said.

The man directed his attention to Sarah. "I know what you hold. The keys. If you have them, you must know the truth."

"It's you again," Sarah said. "Who are you?"

"My name's Ivo." He tried to maintain his composure.

"Let's get out of here, Sarah," Leif said quickly. "He may have helped, but he's not on our side."

Her brain felt like it was going to burst. She felt woozy and weak. Sides. What did he mean by sides?

"If it wasn't for me, you wouldn't have known how to control this stardust surge from the pond," he said with confidence. "I know who you are. Let's talk about you." Ivo stood directly in front of Leif.

Leif pulled Sarah up. "Please go back to your house, Sarah." He then faced Ivo. "It doesn't matter who I am."

"You work for him, you're one of Panveer's agents. Your dad is, at least," Ivo said. "Be careful who you are listening to, Sarah. If your name really is Sarah." His voice spat out the last word. *Her name.*

He backed up and ran back down the trail, into the forest.

"You have no idea what's going on here. No idea!" Leif shouted, fists clenched.

Leif turned toward Sarah. "Let's get out of here, you're probably freezing."

"He's the weird guy that I was telling you and Tindra about. He followed me and told me all that stuff." She lingered for a while and watched him as he disappeared into the forest.

"Weird is right." Leif put his jacket around Sarah.

"Thanks." She shivered. "But maybe he can help us? Maybe he can help me with these keys. All the stuff he told me before, maybe it isn't so crazy anymore."

Leif didn't say anything. He pulled out his phone and looked through some messages. "If anyone is going to help you, it's not him."

"Leif, now would be a good time to tell me what you know. You said that there is more about this place." She looked over at the pond, completely quiet as it was before. She shivered again in the cold. "Why did the keys come to me?"

Leif watched her speak but didn't respond.

"Or maybe I am just crazy." Sarah exhaled and spun around. "My grandfather was right, always reminding me about the accident. It's what makes me see things. It's what …" She felt tears of exhaustion fall from her eyes.

Sarah reflected as she shivered, her damp sweater cold against her skin. Her head pounded even more. "But I … I don't care, Leif." She looked at him, tears in her eyes. "It's too confusing. My migraines get heavier and stronger each time this strange stuff happens. Seeing the lights in the trees back in Maine, seeing what just happened here. And even the keys. I feel like they are making it all worse."

"Follow me. We need to bring these keys to someone." He took her hand, took the keys out of them and placed them in her pocket, zipping it up. "My dad is expecting us. We need to go now."

"Your dad? What does he want with them?" she asked, surprised.

"I don't have authority to say yet. I ..." Leif struggled with his words.

"Authority?" Sarah questioned. Her voice was weak and strained.

"There's more about ... everything, Sarah." Leif looked around. "I have taken an oath of secrecy. It's ..."

She looked at him. So many questions were in her mind.

Leif walked her up to the driveway of her Aunt Gale's house.

As they approached, Gale opened the door and stepped out, "Come on in, quickly now." She paused. Sarah walked past her into the house. "Leif, join us. We could see everything from here, the lights ... We were just going to run out but then we got your message." She looked at Leif.

"You two know each other?" Sarah asked.

Leif followed Gale into the house and Sarah watched him.

He ignored her question. "All your life, haven't you been wondering why you're different? Why do you have the ability to see things that others do not? And now, now it is revealed that you have the powers we've been waiting for," Leif explained.

"We? Who's we?" She looked at Gale for support. Gale smiled and stepped forward.

"We just came from the gazebo and the pond," Sarah told her. "It shot up, like with all this strange energy, and I don't know how, I ..."

Henrikson walked in from the living room, the man who had been with her aunt the other day.

"Hi again, Sarah." He paused. "We didn't mention it to you before, but I'm Leif's dad."

"What is going on here?" Sarah backed up into the kitchen. "Why are you here?"

"This whole thing, this move to Walton, it's brought us all to this moment to reveal the truth to you. You are significant, you are necessary, and you have found the keys that have been missing," Henrikson explained. "This is more important than you'll ever know."

"The keys," Sarah whispered. Her head pounded.

"There's more than just what you see, Sarah," Gale continued. "You see … this world. This world that we are in is just one realm within the Startrail. The Startrail is the universe, and there are more realms. Sarah, these realms are only accessed through Portal Paintings."

"You knew all of this, but you didn't tell me?" Sarah looked at her aunt with grilling eyes. Sarah backed up and sat down on a chair. "Portal Paintings." She thought back to the strange painting that she saw in her house. "I remember." She squeezed her eyes shut and pressed her hand against her head to ward off the migraine pain.

All their eyes were glued on her.

"At my house, before I came here, I remember seeing the painting, a strange painting. It seemed to just show up. And …" She paused, feeling lightheaded. "And when I touched it, my hand … it went …"

"Through it?" Gale finished her sentence. "That was one of the agents' paintings, when they were—"

"There was an agent in my house!?" she shouted. Her heart was beating hard.

"Means to an end, dear. Once you know everything, you'll see." Gale paused. "We feel that you have displayed the necessary powers to create these worlds. You may be a Portal Painter. The power that came through you at the gallery? It's not imagined," Gale continued.

"You told them?" she quietly asked Leif.

"He works for us. He may be a student at Walton High, but he is also on an important mission that's bigger than all of us, than all of this," Gale shared.

"Your dad's company," Sarah whispered. "This is the company? Is it some sort of cult?"

Gale moved towards Sarah. "It's the reality of everything and everyone around us. It will seem like a cult because you've never heard about it before." She smiled. "You must open your mind."

"We want you to try painting again, and with the right tools, you can help us. You can help us gain access into the Painter's Keep," Henrikson said.

She shook her head and closed her eyes. "My head." She leaned forward, pressing her hand against her forehead. "The migraines."

"Maybe she needs some water," Leif suggested.

Sarah felt angry at Leif for not telling her the truth. "Don't pretend you care, Leif. You work for them."

"I tried to tell you outside—I'm under oath," Leif said.

Henrikson stepped forward, a bottle in his hand. "Gale, here."

She looked up at Henrikson with worry in her eyes. "Are you sure?"

"It's what is used in times like this. Migraines and such. Just like a regular painkiller," he continued.

Sarah's mind went back to when the strange man, Ivo, came over to her and told her about this Painter's Keep. She felt like she was in the middle of a bad dream.

"You can't deny that there has to be a reason for everything that you've seen and experienced in your life." Leif's father sat next to her and looked into her eyes. "This is your purpose, Sarah."

Gale looked on proudly. "It must sound strange. Most people of Earth Realm would never give any of what we are saying a moment's thought. But you … you have finally seen it, and we now see that you have it in you."

"Why wouldn't I remember this?" She closed her eyes,

keeping the pain at bay. "I mean, shouldn't I remember?" She stood up, ignoring the pain. "This is all too weird. It makes no sense at all. Please, please just leave me alone."

The man fumbled with the bottle and an orange pill dropped out into his hands. Her mind flashed to her father's pills. Was she becoming her father? Would she begin to black out? Not be in control? Maybe she needed to take it.

"The accident, Sarah," Gale reminded her.

She shook her head. "How could a collision just erase all knowledge of this reality you speak of?"

No one responded. She thought of her father, deep in contemplation; he was always trying to remember something. Anything. Something from before.

"Creating worlds?" she struggled to say through the pain. After a minute of deep breathing, the pangs from the migraine let up, a little and her vision became clearer. Henrikson handed her the pill.

"If you thought this could be, why didn't you tell me before?" She looked at Gale.

"The keys weren't missing, and so we didn't find it necessary to tell you. But now … now things are different, and we desperately need your help," Gale shared. "We knew it would be hard for you to hear this. To understand."

"But why is my dad in jail?" Sarah shouted. "Does it have anything to do with all of this?"

"Your dad being in jail was out of our control."

"Why would I help you?" Sarah looked up into the man's eyes. "I came out here to be with family, family that I hardly know, but I thought I could trust, at least. But little did I know you were all waiting and watching for me to do something."

There was a silence that followed. She continued, "I don't want that pill. I don't want anything you give me."

"Once you know the reason for your existence, and why

you are the way you are, you will want to help us," Henrikson explained. "And we … we will help you."

"Help me with what?" Sarah asked.

"We will do all that we can to get your dad out of jail." Henrikson shared, his face was motionless and his eyes were looking down.

Sarah's heart suddenly lifted.

Henrikson continued, looking her straight in the eye. "But … *we will need you to help us find something first.*"

CHAPTER 14

Stanley felt grass under his back; the air was warm, and it felt like summer. He sat up and saw it, the necklace, it sparkled in her hand. She was sitting right next to him, laughing, her ashy hair wavy down her back, and he was smiling at her. Stanley felt peace like it was a tangible thing. The woman was painting something and the paint she was using made things move; the pictures were moving. He couldn't understand what he was seeing, and the drowsiness was starting. "Stanley, please hold this." She spoke so smoothly. "The power in this will get us through the seafaen. If necessary, we can use this." Her voice was muffled and quiet, almost like she was mouthing the words. "The keys are going to have to be hidden. He may try to take them. He's been acting strange." Sorrow was nestled in her eyes. He didn't understand it, but did he remember it? Then, it was like his eyes were so heavy he couldn't stay awake, and the next time he opened them, the grass was gone, and the only things surrounding him were three concrete walls, and bars. He had passed out on the bed in his cell.

He blinked a few times and struggled to regain consciousness. He pressed his hands against his eyes, leaving them damp. Was he crying? He stood up fast. "See-fayne." He spoke the word quietly to himself. The sharp pain in his head began, as it usually did after he had a vision. He fumbled around for the one notepad and pencil that he had with him and wrote down what he could remember: *Hold this. Seafayne? Seafaen? Power in this will get through. Hide the keys. Long dark blond hair.*" He threw it down by his pillow and exhaled. What did any of that mean? Were these all memories, or just random hallucinations? He clung to what Dr. Yun had said about him not going crazy.

One of the guards walked up to the cell. "You have a visitor."

It wasn't Sarah's visiting day, but maybe she'd decided to come early. It's a school week though, he reasoned. They brought him downstairs to the visiting area with the glass that divided prisoners and guests.

A very tall man, with darker skin and dark curling hair stood in front of him. He was wearing a suit and had the look of a lawyer. Stanley felt a sense of relief.

He tried to keep things light, "So I'm guessing you are my lawyer?" He laughed expectantly.

The man didn't say anything.

Feeling uncomfortable, Stanley got right to the point. "Who are you?"

"Don't tell me you don't know who I am. It may have been ten years, but I haven't aged that much, have I?"

If he was trying to be funny, Stanley couldn't detect it.

"I'm here about the fate of … you know what." He looked around carefully. "I finally found you. I … I knew you'd be here somewhere. Somewhere in this strange realm."

Stanley noticed the prison guard looking at him curiously. Stanley looked at him suspiciously too. Realm? What did he mean by realm? This was strange talk for a lawyer.

"What do you mean you've been looking for me everywhere?" he said. "Listen, you've got to help me. I didn't do this. I will admit that I was at the pawnshop, but it was closed. But then, the door was open at the back, and so I went in. And that's when it happened." Stanley rubbed his head.

The man interrupted him. "I don't care what you did. We'll get you out of here. I am just amazed I found you." He looked around carefully and whispered very quietly, hoping the guard didn't hear, "We need you back with the team. The Startrail is in dire times."

Stanley closed his eyes as if it would help the pang of his migraine go away. The word "Startrail" clanked in his brain. The man looked strangely familiar, like he'd seen him somewhere in a dream or one of his visions, or maybe in a movie. He couldn't pinpoint it.

"So, are you my lawyer?" Stanley's eyes were bloodshot and heavy. He closed them and then opened them again, only to see the door to the communication room swing open. Another man in a suit came in. He was short and stocky with dark hair and a beard.

"Lawyer?" the second man said. "No, no. I am your lawyer." He looked the other man up and down. "I don't know who this guy is."

The tall, dark-haired man stood up. "I never said I was his lawyer. I am an old friend. Believe me, Stannach, I will do what I can to get you out of here." He glanced at the stocky man and continued. "I know it's been a decade, but it's me, Viggo! Where's your daughter? Is she OK?"

"What do you want with my daughter? Of course, she is fine." Stanley said, tired from all the confusion.

"What is with you, Stannach? Don't you remember? Don't you remember anything? To speak with you frankly, the keys are missing, but we believe that they have made their way into Earth Realm." His eyes were kind, they didn't look conniving or deceitful. Could Stanley have known this guy?

The short man looked at Viggo again and then turned toward Stanley. "Ignore whatever that man said. He's obviously out to lunch. Hi, Stanley, I'm your lawyer, Edgar Havensworth."

He looked at the guards. "You may wish to check this man's credentials. Does he have permission to be seeing my client? Mr. Carlson has an appointment with his lawyer. That's who I am." He emphasized the "I".

The guards motioned towards Viggo. "Come with us, sir. We'll need to see ID." Viggo was reluctant to leave; he looked back at Stanley, hopeful that he would remember.

Stanley wanted to remember. How nice it would have been to have a friend come and visit. He briefly remembered the vision he'd had of the woman who spoke about keys. Maybe this was a friend from before his accident. But he couldn't just trust him and hope he was telling the truth. It felt like something was tearing within Stanley's brain again. It was pulling at his brain like it wanted to reveal itself, like it had a life of its own. He leaned forward and pressed his hands to his head. The guards came to help and immediately escorted Viggo out of the room.

"I think I need my medication." He then turned back toward the man. "And I'd like to talk to that guy. Please." Again, something panged in his brain. He wanted to grin and bear it, he wanted to pull through, but the migraine was too strong. "I think he can help me. Please."

"Listen to me. You've got to pull yourself together. Ignore that guy, he's talking nonsense." A vein twitched in Edgar's forehead. It was as if his eyes could laser their way through the glass. "I don't know how that man got in here."

"If you're really my lawyer, then you need to get that man

back in here. I think he may be an old friend from before the accident," Stanley said.

"I see, I see. Well. For now, I came to tell you that your trial has been postponed for a few more months."

"What, why?!" Stanley shouted with the few ounces of energy he had left.

"Well, we have yet to discover more evidence in your favor, Stanley. But as your lawyer, I promise you will be heard, and I will build your side of the story, with your help. But we won't be doing this for another couple of months." Edgar leaned back. Stanley sat there in confusion. It wasn't fair. He didn't do the crime, he should not have to be behind bars at all. Whoever set this up will pay, he thought.

"Our firm is busy this time of year. Waiting isn't always a bad thing. It will give you time to pull your thoughts together to build your case." Edgar looked at his phone. "Looks like I have another meeting." He shot up from the stool that he was sitting on. "Good to meet you, Mr. Carlson."

There was something in his eyes that Stanley didn't like. "Wait!" Stanley bashed his hands on the counter in front of his chair out of frustration. "Wait! Please!"

His lawyer was gone. How could he explain his experiences, how could he get his story to the right people? He felt like he could break through the clear window with his anger alone. He breathed deep and saw the security guard motioning for him that it was time to go. All he had was time—time in this cage. Caged for a reason that wasn't true. The only thing he could do was get his story straight. The word "Startrail" crashed into his mind repeatedly. What was it about that word? He needed to start remembering, and he needed to do it fast. He needed to stop the medication.

CHAPTER 15

Sarah was sitting on a chair in the kitchen, trying to ward off the headaches. She held the painkiller from Henrikson in her hand.

"Come with us," Henrikson said. "We will show you more—more of what we are talking about."

The only thing that made her willing to follow Henrikson and Gale was the fact that there finally could be an answer to all her questions about her life. She was desperate for any sort of meaning. They walked out into the night, into the forest trail. Sarah was behind Henrikson and Gale, who led the way. Leif was quietly walking beside Sarah.

"I don't know why you didn't tell me before," Sarah said under her breath.

"I couldn't. Not until …" Leif hesitated. He stopped and looked her in the eye. "Not until we knew that you held the power."

"So, that's all I am to you, someone who holds this power?" Sarah shook her head and kept walking forward. "How do you think I feel that all my life I've been lied to?

And someone who I thought—" She stopped walking and looked at him briefly.

"I know." He looked down. "I didn't know you'd be so great. I'm sorry. I mean it."

"Leif, let's go," Henrikson called out to him.

Sarah could tell that Leif meant what he was saying, and although she was angry with him, it wasn't only him. It was everyone, it was the secrecy that made her mad. Henrikson stopped and turned to his right. There was nowhere to go except down a neatly spaced trail, with heaving evergreens on each side. The shimmer in the trees was more apparent than ever as they walked down the trail.

She felt the ground. The fall leaves that covered the pathway were gone and it was all soft moss.

"What is this?" she whispered to herself. The mossy path led down to the edge of the ocean. But from her knowledge of Walton, the coast was still a mile or two away.

"This makes no sense." Sarah looked up and out. Something drew her forward. The coast was not the Walton coast. There was no island, there was no lighthouse. It was just pure glistening water, completely still. Like glass. The mossy pathway ended when she came upon a sandy shore.

"Where is this?" She looked at Leif. "I went down this trail before, but never have I seen this."

"Yeah, I know." Leif laughed. "Remember the day I met you at school, when you were coming out of the trail?"

She recalled how the trail had seemed so mysterious.

"This is a realm within a realm," Henrikson proudly exclaimed. Gale smiled at him and watched Sarah's face for her reaction.

"A what?" Sarah looked at Leif. She was in awe. "This can't be real."

"It is real. It must seem strange, but this is reality."

"So, have other people in Walton come through here?"

"Only those with knowledge of the Startrail, and enough stardust within them, or with them, can enter."

"How did I get in then?"

Leif laughed. "You have no idea."

"What do you mean?"

"How powerful you really are."

"We got in because we have built up enough stardust within ourselves. It's our profession, we live it, breathe it, and travel in it," Henrikson said.

Sarah didn't respond. She bent down to feel the water. Where was this place? She tried to think of answers that would make sense, but she couldn't think of anything. Her finger tapped the water and it sent out a ripple atop the vast expanse of ocean. The ocean looked as clear as the sky and the sky looked as clear as the ocean. For a moment she felt dizzy and out of sorts. She looked down onto the glassy water and her face stared back at her. Her hair was shimmering with an otherworldly sheen. Her eyes were brighter than before, and she was smiling. Sarah wasn't smiling though. She looked up, falling backwards, shocked at what she had seen. It was her, but it wasn't her. She, herself, was doing something else. She looked in again. The face in the water was still smiling, as if it had a mind of its own. And then she was looking at herself, looking up from the water, as if she was smiling at something or someone.

"Walton is one of the few places in Earth Realm that has storehouses of stardust. It's hidden from most people. But not us, we know where it is," Gale said proudly.

"This is why people were saying that the owner of this land wouldn't sell it." Sarah made a connection.

"This place is exceptionally valuable because these storehouses are right in the backyard allowing access to realms, hidden places. Mere earth dwellers will always have a hard time understanding that; it could never be bought or sold." Henrikson replied.

"Some folklore might attribute all this to magic or secret worlds, only found in fairy tales and the like," Gale continued. "But they are very real realms connected to a very real fact: that stardust contains power that links realms. Creating the Startrail."

When Sarah looked at her blankly, Gale went on.

"The Startrail is like what you'd call the universe. It is different realms all connected by Portal Paintings. Given life and energy and vitality by stardust. Not just stardust as you may know it. It's more powerful than that. Stardust, in a liquid form called seafaen, is used to create a powerful paint that will create portals into other realms."

Sarah didn't respond; she was trying to take it all in.

"You'll understand in due time," Gale said. "But you, you probably have an ability that we don't. You can see the stardust. You may be able to see it collecting in certain places where star pockets or hidden realms within realms, like this one, are found."

Gale struck a chord with her for once. "I think I know what you are saying. All my life I have been able to see a shimmering substance at various times, in some forested areas."

"Only in certain forests, right?" Gale added.

"Yeah, only in—" Sarah paused.

"Two?" Gale finished her sentence.

"Yeah. But why didn't you say anything before?"

"We didn't know you had the power. We thought you might just be like everyone else in Earth Realm," Henrikson jumped in.

She looked to her left and right. The coast extended as far as the eye could see; the water was perfectly still, perfectly clear, and serene. The coast was different than in Walton. It had to be a dream. It had to be her imagination. They walked along the shore.

"So you guys have been watching me?" Sarah asked. "Waiting for me to display power?"

"No," Gale quickly said. "We were going on with life as usual. But when you were sent out here, we noticed that you showed the signs."

"The keys, Sarah," Henrikson said. "Now that we are here, let's view the keys."

She had put the keys in her pocket again when Leif gave them back to her; she brought them out slowly. They glistened softly. "Here. They won't let me leave them anywhere. Every time I walk away, they follow me."

"Interesting." He looked at Gale.

"Is there a reason for that?" Sarah asked Henrikson.

"It confirms that you have the powers that we have been keeping watch for. We are the United Ones of the Startrail. It's a team of people who are on a mission to ensure realms have enough stardust," Henrikson shared.

"There is a lack of stardust here, a lack of power, in other words. Power to keep Earth Realm within the network of realms," Gale added. "And these keys—they will help bring access to the seafaen waterfalls within the Painter's Keep. It will help us to keep Earth Realm and other realms active, lest they lose it all and are destroyed."

"Destroyed? How can the Earth be destroyed?" Sarah said in almost a whisper.

"Follow me," Henrikson said, ignoring her question. He stood at the edge of the water and held out a hand. "We will take the keys to a safe place."

Immediately, a contraption appeared above them as if by magic. It was an open gondola. The vessel lowered to the ground and he stepped in, and the others followed. Leif held out his hand to Sarah, who hesitated on the shore.

He nodded toward her reassuringly.

Once she was in, the gondola zipped them up and over the waters to another coastline with cliffs and rugged hills. There was a walkway that led into an entrance in the cliff wall. The gondola stopped to let them off, and disappeared again. They walked into the cave-like entrance.

"To the right you'll see the doorway to our headquarters here in Walton, in Earth Realm."

Gale opened the door by raising her hand toward the doorway. "Of course, this wouldn't be visible to the average eye. Remember, it's a realm within the realm. The only way here is through the way we brought you."

Within the headquarters, there were dangling chandeliers and lights. Chairs, tables, and computer systems were set up around the edges of the grand room. Above the computers were windows. At least, they were like windows, but it almost looked like glimpses of space on the walls. Full of glittering stars.

"What you see in front of you are star maps. Not of outer space as you may know it, but reflections of what is going on in the Startrail. There was a great war that occurred a decade ago. Many realms were wiped out. Too many were being created, and there wasn't enough stardust to sustain them."

"How is this even possible? How did I not know about this before?" Sarah gazed around the room. She couldn't ignore it now, it was evident that there was a bigger picture at play, but something still didn't sit quite right.

"I don't want to be involved in any of this," she said in a whisper, her heart pounding.

Leif nodded at people he seemed to know well who were working in the offices. She looked at the art that was on the walls. There were paintings of palaces that held an unearthly beauty. She stopped at one painting. It was a picture of the three keys together, creating a triangle. In the middle there was a light. She stared at it, focusing on the intricate detail. The keys. These were the keys that she had found, and the symbol that she remembered seeing on the necklace in her grandfather's office. It also was on Leif's ring. It was all starting to come together.

This place had to hold the answers that she was searching for—the answers about the keys, about her past, about her life and strange thoughts. People looked at her with intensity. Did they know about her already?

"They have been waiting for you, Sarah," Leif whispered.

"Why … why me?" She looked down at the floor and then into Leif's eyes. "I'll give them the keys and go. I feel weird about all of this."

"Trust me, you're going to want to be a part of this."

Where else would she go? Back to Maine, and wait for her dad to get out of jail? Or back to Walton, finish school, and live at Tindra's place? But now she knew that somehow Tindra's family was a part of this thing too, so she wouldn't want to stay there.

Henrikson's words were starting to blur together. The agonizing thought that she was forgetting something, that she was missing something, was still grinding at her mind. The information that she had gathered still didn't bring her the peace she was looking for, not when her father was still in jail. She wondered if Henrikson would help her father, like he said. How could he do it? How would he have the power?

She followed Henrikson and Gale into a circular room, stone walls all around. There was a large window over-looking the ocean. She looked out the window that jutted out over the steep cliff. Her heart could have jumped out of her throat. The thought of this place being in a different realm within Earth Realm was too difficult to conceive.

A table suddenly emerged from the floor. A beautiful

starry scene could be seen on the surface of the table, just like the star maps that she had seen in the first room.

"Panveer. We have daughter Sarah Carlson here."

"Daughter?" Sarah whispered.

Leif leaned toward her. "They call everyone sons and daughters."

"Of who?"

"Sons and daughters of the United Ones." Leif shared under his breath.

Henrikson looked at Leif with serious eyes. "Quiet."

Leif straightened up and focused on the table.

"She is here with the keys."

There was no response.

Sarah felt uneasy. Were they trying to summon a spirit? Were they talking to themselves? Who was Panveer? She remembered the strange man, Ivo, mentioning the name, and that Henrikson worked for him, but who was he, really?

"She has the keys to the Painter's Keep."

"Henrikson, Panveer is in Blue Veil. He is collaborating with the Panthers there. Is it true? The keys are with you?" the voice said.

She wondered what they meant by "Panthers."

"Yes, she is here, and the keys are with her."

"All three?"

There was a pause.

Gale looked nervously at Henrikson. She spoke up. "I'm afraid there are only two."

"The storehouses are running low. You must find the third key. If not, there will be many realms dismantled. Survival will depend on it."

"Yes, we know." Henrikson's voice was grim.

He looked at Sarah. She had never felt such pressure. There had to be a third key, the symbol showed that, and the visions did too. How was she to know where the third key would be? Was it up to her?

As if sensing Sarah's nerves, Leif's hand reached over and took hers. She looked over at him, feeling a sense of ease, and nerves at the same time. Now wasn't the time for romance, but she couldn't help but think about him. Even during strange circumstances, his presence was strong and calming.

"She has no recollection of the Startrail and so this has been a unique experience for her."

There was talking heard in the background.

"Earth Realm must be evacuated within the next few days," the voice continued. "Panveer has sent word that due to the shortage we must follow through with the plan unless the third key is found in time. If the third key is found, then Earth Realm can be properly restored."

Sarah's head began to hurt again. Fear started to bubble, that old familiar feeling that she hated. The nerves she felt like she couldn't control. And yet a voice in her mind was reminding her that *there is more*. This seemed to be *the more* that she had been looking for. The keys, the strange visions. This could now be her purpose, as foreign as it was.

"It will appear to her as the others have."

They all looked at Sarah strangely. She wanted to speak up, but she didn't know what she would say.

Leif let go of her hand once the talking stopped.

The table went into the floor again and they left the room and walked into a place with chairs. There were few windows. The sky outside was dark.

"Please everyone, let's sit down." Gale sat on an emerald couch across from Leif and Henrikson. Sarah sat next to her. A tall woman with hair perfectly pulled back into a bun swiftly walked over to deliver some sort of beverage. It was warm and in copper mugs.

"Apple cider, sir." She gave a sort of bow toward

Henrikson before she left.

Henrikson took the mug and lifted it toward his nose. He breathed it in. "Thank you, Celia. Try some, Leif and Sarah."

Gale looked at Henrikson curiously. "This is infused with rationed stardust. There is only so much that we can have access to at this time. Panveer always ensures that we are fully stocked in every realm. The last few years, however, have been more difficult."

"You can drink it?" Sarah asked hesitantly.

"Oh yes. It helps bring energy, vitality, and restores your thought processes," Gale said as she took a sip. Leif followed. Sarah watched him sip. There was something that flashed in his eyes—a slight flash of black—and then it was gone.

Sarah took a sip. It was the most delicious apple cider that she had ever tasted. It was tart but sweet and infused with thick cinnamon aroma. She felt the same as before, but they all looked at her carefully as if they expected something else, something important to happen.

"What do you think?" Henrikson asked.

"It tastes great."

"That's all?" Leif said.

Gale continued, "It will allow your mind to see where the stardust is. You see, in this place, it is all around us."

Sarah didn't know how to respond to that. "I'm sorry, I don't think I know what you mean."

Henrikson looked at Celia with concern.

She stepped forward. "I assure you, sir, we used the usual cider."

"Oh well, it's because Sarah already has the unique ability to see the stardust where it is, she just isn't able to hone that skill yet." They all listened intently. "The shimmer of lights you see in the forests—only certain forests, of course—it's stardust. And there are few places left in Earth Realm that have these stardust-saturated areas."

Sarah looked around at everyone bustling about in the stone cliffside hideout. They moved around with such purpose, intensity.

"Sarah," Henrikson began the conversation, "as you heard in the circular room, we will have to evacuate Earth Realm. There hasn't been enough stardust in these areas and since we haven't access to the Painter's Keep, we will need to leave. You need to find the other key. If you find it, then we will be able to access the Painter's Keep and retrieve the seafaen used for the portal paintings."

"Can you find it, Sarah? Can you find the other key?"

Leif shifted in his seat, awaiting Sarah's response.

"I don't know what to say." Her head panged. She looked up at Leif and then the others. "It's not like I sought out these keys. They just came to me. They just appeared."

"Which is why the third one must appear to you soon, one would hope," Gale noted nervously. "If they are being sent to her specifically, in the way that we think."

Leif interrupted, mid sip, "What way is that?"

"They weren't supposed to be sent. They were sent without any permission and in a complex way. We will not discuss that any further."

Leif looked stifled and leaned back

"I know you all want me to help," said Sarah, "but all of this has been a lot to take in, and something that I don't think I want to be part of."

Henrikson spoke up. "Don't go making assumptions or forming any type of opinion on all of this yet. You don't know the facts. We will show you everything about the Star-trail. Leif will guide you and help you."

Leif smiled at her. Surprisingly, it was enough to reassure her in the moment.

"The keys can stay in here. We can help you not to feel like they are attached to you," Henrikson continued.

Sarah took out the keys and laid them out in the palms of her hands. The words *protect the keys* came over her again. Maybe this was a way to protect them. Gale exhaled when she took them into her hands, as if all her life she had waited for this one moment, the return of the keys.

If anything, Sarah would be glad to leave all this strange stuff behind and start new somewhere else. She could then focus her attention on getting her father out of prison. Her mind drifted to all that could be. She could get an apartment some place in Augusta and visit her father every day, go to school to become a lawyer, and fight to get him out.

She watched the keys glisten in Gale's hands. A flash of regret zoomed through her heart as Gale handed them to Henrikson, who placed them in a bag. He then took out a long vase with a diamond-like cork that sealed what was inside within. The liquid inside the vase shimmered slightly. He looked at Sarah as if he wanted to explain what it was, but whatever he was doing was urgent enough to bypass all information or explanations. There was an eagerness in his eyes and a quickness in his hands.

"Leif, open the bottle for me."

Leif did as he was told and pulled the seal off the bottle. Sarah couldn't help but think that the vase and liquid looked familiar. Her mind immediately flashed to the hands holding it, and then holding the keys, the voice saying to protect the keys. The vision. Did her past vision lead her to this moment? Did it relate? She closed her eyes for a moment.

Then she re-opened them to see Henrikson pouring the liquid into the bag that had the keys in it.

"Now they are coated."

"With what? What is that?" Sarah asked.

"Seafaen," Gale said. "It will keep the keys from constantly being brought toward you. Seafaen is an ingredient vital to all of life within the Startrail. It allows people to fly, it allows people to travel into other realms, and most importantly, it allows the Portal Painters to paint exquisite new worlds."

"Seafaen can also be used to cloak things, hide things. Have you ever heard of a seafaen wall?" Leif asked.

"No."

"It's when seafaen is wielded to create a barrier around something, to hide it, and protect it!" Leif explained.

"You can see this bag and so can we, but when the seafaen coating was applied to the keys as a cloaking protection, then it also hid them from view."

"When will they be hidden?" Sarah asked.

"They're hidden now. You can see them, of course, which is why you are unique," Gale continued. "This is why you are special. And you are now part of this team. We thank you for bringing the keys to us."

"See?" Henrikson opened the bag to reveal the keys covered in the glowing liquid coating. "Can you see the keys?"

"Yes."

"And that's it!" He smiled, which was something she noticed he didn't do often. "You can see things that we cannot."

A sense of relief came over Sarah as she realized that finally someone understood her ability to see things. Finally there was a reason for all the strange happenings.

"They will be kept away from all eyes. But the bag allows us to know where they are, since the cloaking hides them," Henrikson said swiftly. "It's for the best. One day you'll see just how important these artifacts are."

"When the other one comes to you, bring it to us and then we can be on our way."

"I don't understand why these keys are coming to me in the first place."

"It's a mystery that only the Startrail will reveal."

"It's a lot to take in." Sarah looked down. "Maybe my father has been trying to remember his past for very good reasons. Not just for average memories, but the reality of all this …"

Gale nodded, she looked at Henrikson. "Just because you have been chosen doesn't mean your father or grandfather would know anything about the Startrail."

Sarah thought for a moment, but then added, "Yeah, but he's been saying some crazy things lately. Maybe he knows something."

"That is something we will need to think about later. For now, let's focus on what we need to do next. We believe you have the skill of seeing the invisible. This ability you have will help us immeasurably. Certain things that have been hidden or stolen from us over the years cannot be found because only a few have the skills to find them."

Gale leaned forward. "There is a necklace."

"It's been missing for years, and it holds a lot of power," Henrikson said. "It looks like this."

He reached into his pocket and pulled out a picture. It was a picture of the exact same necklace that Sarah remembered her grandfather receiving and wearing.

"How did it go missing?" Sarah asked. " I'm pretty sure my grandfather had some sort of special necklace. There's a picture of him wearing it and my father became obsessed with finding it, right before he was put in jail. This is why I think he might know something about the Startrail too."

There was silence for a brief moment as if Sarah had revealed too much.

Gale finally spoke up, "I don't think he would know, but it is a necklace of high value that has been passed around, and it may have landed in your grandfather's hands because it was bought and then he sold it. You see, enemies of the Startrail took it. For years it's been missing, and it's vital to the

Startrail's survival. It will help us access the storehouses of stardust for times such as this."

"Whoever took the necklace must have placed a seafaen cloaking over it, making it invisible to most people, which is why you are so valuable. You will be able to see where it is." Henrikson continued.

A part of her still felt like she was in a dream, or like everyone was acting out a play in front of her. How could this all be real? She had gone from being an ordinary student to talking about seeing invisible things, talking about magical necklaces and keys. Then again, it also made so much sense. She had been thirsting for more all her life, and now, this was *the more.*

"You said, enemies of the Startrail," Sarah said slowly. "So my dad and my grandfather, could they be ..."

Gale jumped in. "I know your grandfather, he isn't the Startrail type. When I was introduced to it, I tried to share, but he didn't want anything to do with it. Your father was the same, and then the accident happened which made it worse to even bring up the subject." Gale paused. "This is why you and I share something special—the desire to know what is really out there, what is really true."

Something about what Gale had just said was comforting and yet conflicting at the same time. Her father being the enemy of anything seemed hard to believe.

"You said that you could help my dad, right?" Sarah said.

There was a hesitation. Leif looked at both of them and at Sarah.

"Yes, we can help your dad. We have ways to get him out of jail," Henrikson said. Sarah couldn't help but smile. "But you need to get this necklace for us, Sarah. Not only the necklace but the other key. It is important. For all of us, for the United Ones." He paused and lowered his solemn voice. "It benefits us all."

"So, tell us, Sarah," Gale leaned forward again. "Where do you think this necklace could be?"

Sarah explained how she thought it was in the pawnshop back in Augusta.

"Tomorrow we will go to Maine. We can stay in our apartments there and Sarah will help us locate the necklace." Henrikson hesitated as he turned to Sarah. "And then, we will retrieve your father."

"We have further discussions that will not require your presence," Henrikson said to Leif. "Wait by the front."

"Sure," Leif replied.

Once Sarah was alone with Leif, she turned to him. "Are there any Portal Paintings here?"

"Yeah, there are."

"Please can we go see them?" she begged.

"They hold profound power."

Sarah followed Leif down a long hall that had rooms on each side. "This is as close as we should get right now. The power is strong and since you're not trained up yet, it could pull you in."

They walked slowly, peering into each room. Every room was empty except for one painting on the wall. She could feel what Leif was saying, some sort of pull that came from within the rooms, within the paintings. Leif stood right beside her as they slowly walked down the hall. She grabbed his arm, suddenly feeling fearful at the thought of being pulled into a portal.

He smiled at the gesture. "Once you are trained, you'll never be afraid, and you'll look back at this moment and laugh, at yourself."

"What do you mean?"

"Nevermind." Leif stopped himself. He appeared embarrassed. "It's just that, if you truly knew how powerful you really are, you wouldn't be clinging onto my arm."

"I'm not clinging…" She looked down and slowly loosened her grip on Leif's arm.

"Nonetheless, no matter how powerful you are, just know that I always have your back. My protection. Even if you won't want it in the future."

They both stopped in the hallway and looked at eachother, her hand on his forearm reached down to his hands and held them for a moment. She felt her heart melt as they stood there and yet she didn't have the words to respond. If she was truthful with herself, she felt like she needed him or needed someone, someone to guide and protect her. The power within her and around her was too strong and she didn't know how to tame it. "Even though I still have yet to understand what you are talking about, I'm glad of that." She laughed.

They continued walking down the hall, hand in hand. She didn't know everything about Leif, but she trusted him, and felt safe.

"How was that other guy able to stop the inverted pond?" Sarah asked. "Is that what you mean by training? If I accidentally caused the pond to do that, then I could learn to stop it too?"

"Yeah—it's the ability to manipulate the flow of stardust, in a way," Leif explained. "It's with your mind, but only certain people can do it."

Sarah wondered if Leif was able to do it.

"Here we are. This is where some of the most important Portal Paintings are stored." She stood in awe at the doorway looking in. It was a bigger room than the others and there were shelves upon shelves of books lining the walls. Leif looked at her, a flash of excitement in his eyes.

The paintings glistened from a distance. Sarah could feel the strange pull toward them. "So, these portal paintings, you can actually go through them?"

"Well yeah, that's how we got here." It all was so obvious for him, she thought, which made sense. He lives in and understands this reality.

"Where were you before?" Sarah swallowed, her nerves started rising and her head began to ache. It was such a weird concept to think of someone coming in from another realm through a painting.

"Ordillaz realm, it's the main headquarters for the United Ones," Leif said walking ahead, motioning towards a painting that was labelled in beautiful golden inscribed lettering, *Ordillaz Realm*. He stopped suddenly and looked at her. "I know it's crazy to you, the idea of going through a portal."

"A lot of this sounds strangely familiar, and it's like I am so close to understanding and yet so far. When I think too much about it, my head aches," Sarah said. "So this seafaen is what makes one have the power to paint new realms. If I'd had seafaen at the gallery, maybe I could have done it?"

"Well, yeah. That's why I was so amazed—you obviously have the gift," Leif shared.

"Where do they keep the seafaen?" Sarah asked. "Maybe I could try again."

"They keep it in storehouses within every United Ones headquarters in each realm," he explained.

They walked silently for a few minutes and approached a beautiful painting hanging on a wall, unlike the others that were resting on easels.

"Wow. This one …" Sarah said slowly. "This one is powerful."

"It's the portal to Ocean Sky," Leif said. "Another realm."

"I need to go in there. I feel pulled … I …" Sarah started moving towards it. She pointed at it. "It's the same—the same as the one in Walton."

"Yeah. It is, but that one is a fake. It's a copy."

She moved closer to it and reached out to touch the painting. She felt a similar pull like she had felt when she touched the inverted waterfall.

"Wait! Sarah—you aren't supposed to go in one right now. Stop!" He grabbed her hand.

"My head. It's aching again, Leif." She fell to the ground in front of the painting. She looked up and saw the bright blue sky colors jumping off of the canvas.

"Are you OK?" Leif asked. "Is it the migraines again?"

"Yeah, I think so." She took Leif's hand as he helped her up.

Leif looked at her with concern. "We need to be careful, Sarah. If we go into the portal, we may not be able to come out."

They both stood in front of the painting.

"Have you been in Ocean Sky?" she asked.

"No, I haven't. I'd love to though—they say the people from Ocean Sky are the most kind and exquisite people." He looked over at her.

They heard footsteps behind them. "Hey. What are you doing here? Do you know how dangerous this is? Just the light from the painting is enough to pull you in!" Henrikson shouted.

Sarah and Leif walked toward Henrikson quickly and followed him out of the room. Henrikson turned toward his son, "Leif, what has gotten into you? Keep to your orders. This is a sacred mission."

Leif replied, "I'm sorry, Dad."

Sarah walked ahead and down the hall, allowing them to finish talking.

"Do not get too close. She is powerful and we need her to understand our position lest any of those Ocean Sky Erleon-followers get in the way again." His whisper was forceful and loud enough for her to hear. Sarah leaned against the stone wall of the hall.

Erleon.

And for a reason she didn't understand, she felt a familiar heartache for something she had lost, something from her core, something from before.

Erleon.

LEIF WAS QUIET AFTER THE CONVERSATION WITH HIS DAD. Sarah could tell he was refocused on whatever mission he was on and even though she wanted to ask Leif all about it, she held off. She reflected on the portal paintings that she had seen and felt, they almost seemed alive. It was hard to believe that Leif travelled through one of them to be in Earth Realm. Gale, Henrikson, Leif, and Sarah soon left the head-quarters and made their way back to Gale's house in near silence. The only words spoken were about how Sarah would help them get the necklace and that they would pick up food on the way to Maine. Sarah wondered what would happen to her father if she wasn't able to find the necklace for them. If there was a way for Henrikson to use whatever powers that he had to get her father out of jail, then she would take it. *No matter what.* Her father was her only family. He needed her.

You're the powerful one. She heard a voice in her mind. If she truly could paint a portal, then maybe she would believe it. As far fetched as the concept was, she saw evidence of the portals existing, and was too far in to think otherwise. She yearned to know more.

There were two SUVs with drivers waiting in Gale's drive-way. Sarah grabbed her bag from the house and then they all climbed into the vehicles and started their journey to Augusta.

CHAPTER 16

*S*tanley had another visitor. He hoped it was his lawyer again. Maybe he would get an earlier hearing for his case. He waited anxiously in the room that had the glass window separating him and his visitor. Any hope he may have had about getting out of jail, not to mention the hope of remembering his past, was dwindling like a small flame. He tried to fan it, he tried to remember that he was on the verge of something. A new revelation. This is what he was calling it. He was living on the edge. He wasn't taking his medication, which meant the visions were more frequent. It came with the pain of agonizing headaches and migraines, but the visions were worth it.

He squeezed his eyes shut and shook his head; he pressed the palms of his hands against his eyelids. He knew he looked crazy, or like he was on drugs or something. Pressing his hands up to his eyes brought some sort of relief from his headaches, that's why he did it. The guards never flinched; they were used to his twitches by now.

The door opened and the visitor came in. It was that same guy. Not the lawyer. The guy who claimed to be his friend from way back. The guy who said all those strange things and talked about his daughter.

He swallowed. Hope stirred up within him. Maybe this man could help. But he was confused, because this man had been kicked out and told never to come back. But the guards were still and didn't seem bothered at all.

"Stannach," the man, Viggo, said quickly. He kept fumbling with his watch. "I don't have much time. It was hard enough to get in here." He looked at the guards, but they still didn't flinch; it was as if they didn't notice him at all. "You need to listen to me. We are going to get you out of here as soon as we can get enough of the substance. Or if we find the necklace," he whispered.

"Substance? What do you mean substance? Do you know who set me up? Who sent you here?" Stanley blinked heavily, trying to ward off the aching. "I don't know you. I mean, should I know you?"

"The fairies of the lost forests in this realm told me that you'd be here. I showed them pictures of you. The forest guardians know that Panveer's agents have been in this area. I should not have to spell it out for you." He looked lost and waited for Stanley to jump in with understanding. Stanley stared at Viggo with blank eyes, mid-smile.

He then let out a mocking laugh. "You've got to be kidding me." He stood up and yelled upwards and outwards, as if the whole world could hear him. "Is this all a big joke?"

"Why would I make that up?" Viggo leaned back, confused. "It's only been ten years, but you've become like them here. You've forgotten. You've already forgotten where you come from. The lack of stardust does this to worlds. Does the complete disregard for Erleon make people entirely forgetful?"

Viggo shook his head, an intense sadness seemed to come over him. It was sadness mixed with anger. "That's why this realm is so distant. Distant from Erleon, there's no acknowledgment of Erleon. I mean, come on, you know this deep in your soul, you know that Erleon is where all the stardust comes from, what sustains each realm, come on!"

Stanley was silent. Viggo ran his hand through his hair and then leaned forward, placing his hands on the table in front of him. He slowly looked back up at his confused friend. "And just as they say, the more time you spend here, on Earth, the more you forget. I don't know what they have done to you."

"They? Who's they? The aliens, the fairies? Man, you're funny." Stanley continued to laugh, his headache panging against the pressure of the laugh. "Is this some sort of in-house … in-jail entertainment?" He looked around at all the guards, they were not moving at all, they stayed completely still.

"I don't like this, Stan." Viggo looked like he was trying to be patient. "I feel like you're mocking me." He stood up out of his chair. The guards were still not bothered. "What, you need proof? Here, it's me, Viggo. Your old pal."

He took a picture out of his pocket and pressed it up to the window. Stanley leaned in and looked at it, his eyes widened. He leaned back, almost falling off the stool.

"Who are those people?" he said, his voice shaky. Stanley saw himself in the picture with three other people. Viggo was one of them. "I'm with people I don't even know." He leaned in again. What he saw was illogical, unreasonable. It made no sense. He didn't recognize the other two. Or did he? "Wait. I know her."

"Stannach, of course you do. It's me, you, my wife, Marigold, and that's …" his voice faltered. "That's your wife." His voice was quiet as if he revealed information that he shouldn't have. "Why are you acting like this?"

"Acting? I'm not acting," said Stanley. "I … I don't know

who you are, and now you show me this picture with me in it? With other people I don't even know? Are you trying to rub it in?" Stanley was getting worked up. "This is why my dad promised to never show me pictures from my past. It messes things up, it confuses things."

"Rubbing what in?" Viggo said, surprised.

"The fact that I don't remember anything? Anything from ten years ago, from before the accident!" Stanley's words were like arrows that splattered against the window between them. "Who is that woman? I've seen her before. But you're saying she's my wife? That isn't my wife." He paused. "My wife doesn't look like that. She …" He collapsed back on the stool. "She left us."

Viggo was speechless. "Stannach, this is your wife, Esmerelda. The most powerful Portal Painter that ever was."

"Esmerelda," he said under his breath. His heart felt like it was floating, everything within him hushed in reflection. He had seen the woman before, he had to admit. She had long ash-blond hair and a happy-looking face. He could not pinpoint where he knew her from. She looked so comfortable with him, and he had his arm around her. Then there was the revelation. Another revelation.

"Hold that up again, let me see." He struggled with the words. He didn't want to see the picture, but he desperately needed to see it. "What do you mean, Portal Painter?"

The woman. The woman from the visions. The woman who handed him the necklace in all the visions. She's the one in the picture.

He brought his hand through his hair and swallowed. He could only feel anger and resentment. He hated that his memory had failed him. He felt as if his identity was so flimsy, it could fly away with the wind if he wasn't careful. So, he clung to the small aspects that he knew about himself, he clung to his mundane and simple life like it was all he had, like it was gold in his hands. He clung so hard that what he thought was true was starting to crumble. Who could he turn to for the truth? Was his mind playing games with him? Or was his mind trying its best to remember what had happened before? Staying off the medication must have been giving him new information through the visions, and now this visitor was revealing correlating information.

The woman in the picture was the woman in his vision. The one with the necklace. The one with the happy face. And she looked so much like Sarah.

"Portal Painter. Are you messing with me? She paints new worlds. She …" Viggo looked sympathetic again. "I didn't know you had a bad accident. I didn't know. But, why are you in jail? What happened to the necklace?"

"The necklace? You know about the necklace? It was on my dad's neck, he was wearing it, but he gave it away. That's why I went to look for it at the pawnshop, and I ended up here." He found himself willing to give this man any information that he wanted. There was too much that didn't make sense, and yet, too much that was falling together. He wanted it to keep going.

"Your dad. Your dad, Victor? He's back in Blue Veil," Viggo said carefully. He looked around and then down at his watch. It was a very sleek watch, with no clock face or time on it. Stanley wondered how it worked. "He'll be happy to know you've been found."

"Victor? My dad is Irving," Stanley said. "Maybe you've got the wrong guy." But Stanley knew he didn't. He was in this picture. There was proof of them together. "I need to talk to my dad. My dad. Irving. I need to get the story straight." He was fumbling with his words.

"I just can't believe I found you. It's been so long. We thought you were …" Viggo looked down at his watch and back at the guards who still seemed strangely at ease. "But here you are. Tell me one thing, where is your daughter, Silver? You must know her at least?"

"Silver? I don't know who that is," he said, his voice weak.

"Well, you have a daughter, don't you?" Viggo continued.

Stanley didn't know if he should answer that. He had to do all that he could to protect her.

"What about the necklace? Did you find it?" Viggo looked like he was struggling to find some sort of answer. Stanley understood that struggle.

"No. I don't know where it is. I thought it could be at the pawnshop. Holden's Pawnshop. But I didn't have a chance to look for it. It might still be there." He felt powerless. "Let me see the picture just one more time."

Viggo was still standing up and looked flustered. He placed it reluctantly against the glass while looking down at his watch.

He was starting to get worked up. "Here. Your wife. She's somewhere out there, too, and you've just given up, haven't you? You've decided to forget all about it. To play stupid. You can't do this now, not when the Startrail needs you." He looked back at his watch. "I need to tell you something. We have been notified that Panveer's plan has been stalled. We think he's lost access to the Painter's Keep. Somehow the keys have been lost or perhaps sent to the next-in-line Keeper. Do you know what this means?"

He didn't reply.

"It means your daughter, Silver. She could be the next one in line. She could be a Portal Painter." He paused and his words fumbled. "No one knew you even had a daughter, but there were stirrings about this Silver. Then the fairy confirmed that Esmerelda did have a daughter, with you! But then, she and you both went missing."

"Listen," Stanley said, breathing through his teeth. "Are

you here to get me out of jail or not? I don't know what you are talking about. I'm tired. I'm … really …"

He felt a pang of migraine again. He knew he could take the medication that was in his pocket, but he chose not to. He squeezed his eyes shut and opened them. They were bloodshot; he looked like a wreck. Viggo now had his hands in the air in frustration. He brought them down and put them in his pockets while he paced the room. The watch on his wrist was starting to glow. Stanley stared at it, mesmerized.

Viggo moved toward the window and looked him in the eye. "I'm tired of being patient. I don't have enough time. Please, do what you can to remember. Wake up! Wake up, Stannach Elvenly. Wake up!" He was suddenly distracted by his watch and looked down at it. And with that Stanley blinked and he was alone. No one else was there except for the guards behind him. The man seemed to vanish. The guards were startled too.

"Guess your visitor decided to not show his face. Time's up," the guard said, motioning for Stanley to move toward the door.

"But he was here. Is there someone else?" Stanley's words faltered.

"No, only one visitor," the guard answered dryly.

"Didn't you see the man that I was talking to?" Stanley ventured to ask.

The guards laughed with each other.

"Viggo was in here! Viggo, an old friend!" Stanley was getting riled up.

"You mean last week's visitor, who is banned from this place? You're crazy," the first guard said.

"You should see him when he starts hallucinating in his cell," the other one laughed.

Stanley couldn't take it, the bantering, the jokes, it was all too much. He pushed one guard towards the wall and the other one dove out to stop him.

"You don't know what I have been going through. He was there! He was there!" He felt like he was about to explode. He knew it wasn't a hallucination, he knew it wasn't a vision. Viggo was here.

The guard rammed him against the wall, his face hitting the concrete. Stanley didn't try to fight back. He knew he'd crossed the line. There was no point in trying to explain what he'd seen. It must have been another vision. But it wasn't. Everything around him was very real. He tasted the blood coming from his lip. His face ached from hitting the wall. This was not a vision. The prison was the same dull place, the same guards were doing their jobs. Viggo must have had some ability to show up without being seen. Was he a ghost? Stanley laughed that idea off in his mind.

They put him back in his cell. Evening had arrived. He sat on his bed, leaning against his wall. Hours went by and he let the drowsiness overtake him. Before he submitted to sleep, he blinked twice. Was he seeing things? There was a faint purple light in his cell. Maybe it was a side effect of the migraine that he was having, and the sparkles were just auras. But the light kept moving. It kept floating around him in his darkened cell.

"What is that?" Stanley shouted. "Get away!" He tried to brush the light away with his hand.

"Be quiet in there," another prisoner from a nearby cell barked at him.

"This guy's losing it again."

Another muffled voice said something that Stanley could not understand.

Stanley tried to keep his eyes on the floating light, zipping around. It continuously landed on top of his notepad. He watched intently from his bed, leaning forward enough that he fell to the ground.

"What's he up to now?" The same guy gave an annoyed comment.

He ignored his bruised knees and shuffled over to where the notepad was located. He was so close, so close to the bright light. So close that the light turned into a blurry mess of something. Before he knew it, he was writing something; he was writing something, but he didn't know what it was or the message he was conveying. But he wrote as he drifted in and out of consciousness. All the while, the purple light was still illuminating the paper and not moving while he wrote.

Then he fell asleep.

CHAPTER 17

It was still early in the morning. They made their way to Maine, trying to sleep most of the way. Gale and Henrikson had Leif and Sarah go into one of the vehicles, suggesting that they get some sleep on the drive, and while they discussed plans in the other vehicle. Anthony, who also worked for Henrikson, was their driver.

"So, tell me more about this necklace," Leif said. "You saw your grandfather wearing it—but then your dad took it to the pawnshop to try and sell it?"

"Well, I don't know all about it, but I know that's where my dad got into the altercation that put him in jail." Sarah explained to Leif the memory or vision she'd had of the necklace as they watched the landscape speed by. A thud interrupted their conversation. A raccoon scurried across in front of their vehicle. Anthony shouted. A sign saying *Welcome to Augusta* signaled that they had arrived.

"I was hoping to check in with my grandfather," Sarah said. She hadn't talked to him since the last time he had come to their house, when he was acting so different, the time he drove off in the limo. "If you drop me off at my friend's house, she can drive me. I will meet you at the pawnshop after that."

Anthony was listening in. "Leif, your father says that you must not delay. I don't think this is wise."

"Just at least give me a few minutes at my grandfather's place," Sarah whispered to Leif.

Henrikson and Gale were an hour behind because they had made a few stops without them.

Leif looked down at his phone. It was a text from Gale.

Gale: *Tell Anthony to take you right to the apartment, your father and I need to make another stop.*

"Anthony, Gale just said for us to go to the apartment because they are stopping somewhere. We have time to make our own detour." Leif suggested, smiling at Sarah, knowing this stop would make her happy.

Anthony gave in and drove the extra ten minutes to the seniors' home. It was a light pink, long, one-story building. Sarah jumped out of the car and ran inside.

"Hey, wait up, Sarah!" Leif called out, running after her.

"I just want to see if he's OK. Last time I called, he was out, so I didn't get to talk to him," Sarah explained. They were in front of the main welcoming office. The receptionist was on the phone, facing the other direction.

They waited a few moments, Sarah noticed that Leif looked nervous.

"Sarah, maybe we could check in another time." Leif watched to see if the receptionist would notice them.

"Well, we are here now," she whispered. She continued to walk toward her grandfather's room. "I just want to see him for two minutes. What's the big deal?"

There were people sitting and playing cards; an elderly man was fast asleep on a chair in a hallway. Sarah tried to be inconspicuous as she continued to walk down the hall to where her grandfather's room was. They turned to the right;

there was one more hall they needed to go down. She hadn't been to Grandfather's place for years. He always insisted upon coming to their home; he said he didn't want them to see his puny joke of a room. Still, it was strange that he didn't want them to come to his place. "This is the room. From what I can remember."

Leif was busy with his phone but looked up at the door.

Sarah knocked. "I'll just be a few seconds." She watched as the door creaked open; it wasn't fully latched.

"Hello? Grandfather?" She opened the door all the way, looked in carefully, and stood there for a moment. There was nothing in the room, no clothes, no furniture. "Where is he?" She looked at Leif. "Maybe he changed rooms? This is so weird."

"You're sure that this is the room?" Leif asked.

Sarah tried calling his line. The phone on the floor of the empty room rang. She hung up.

"I … I need to find out where he is," Sarah said, almost whispering, "He was acting so strange a few weeks ago, like he …" Sarah stopped herself. "Now that I think of it."

"Let's go, maybe we can call around to some of his friends." Leif looked into Sarah's eyes.

It was quiet for a moment. She looked around. She hoped her grandfather was OK. Someone was walking down the hallway and peered in.

"There you are. We saw you walk in. Your grandfather moved out, dear."

"Where did he go? He didn't tell us anything!" Sarah said, worry written all over her face.

"We don't know where he went off to. He always kept to himself." The woman looked nervous and sympathetic. "It was part of the arrangement. But that's all I really know."

"What sort of arrangement?" Sarah asked, looking at Leif and back at the receptionist.

"He sort of had special privileges here, but that was only because he had a lot of …" She mouthed the last word, "money," and then looked at the two of them. "You're the granddaughter, aren't you? Let's see if we can find a phone number for him."

"Money? What do you mean lots of money?" Sarah sifted through her memories. She never thought of her grandfather as a rich man.

"Sarah, let's go," Leif urged.

"No, I'd like to know where my grandfather moved to," Sarah insisted.

"He didn't give an address. He just packed up and left. I didn't even see a moving truck," the woman said.

They all walked back to the front entrance and the woman flipped through some paperwork.

"Did he leave any sort of message for me?"

"No, nothing, I am so sorry," the woman said, continuing to look through papers. "I don't even see a phone number. To be honest, we never saw much of him around here."

Sarah didn't respond. She looked at Leif who had sympathetic eyes.

"I feel like I don't have any family anymore. I shouldn't have come here," she said. "I just wanted to see him."

"Maybe he communicated with your dad where he was going," Leif suggested. "Anthony must have told my dad that he stopped over here. My dad sent me a text saying that your grandfather had moved out, so there was no point in stopping."

"Well, Gale should know then. She should know, and if she knew then she should have told me." Sarah said in frustration. "You didn't know, right?"

"I don't think I've ever talked about your grandfather with Gale or Henrikson. Or anyone." He paused before continuing, "But when dad sent me this message, I was surprised too."

They walked out the door. Sarah didn't know what to do next. She felt like her world had collapsed, all that she knew held no meaning anymore. Grandfather was missing, her father was in jail.

Anthony agreed to drive them back to Sarah's house for a quick stop before meeting Henrikson and Gale. As they drove, Sarah frantically texted Stina.

"I feel like I've been away for way too long," Sarah said, as Stina walked down the sidewalk to meet them. They walked together up to Sarah's home.

"James has been asking about you," Stina said. Stina looked at Leif awkwardly, unsure whether she should have mentioned James.

For a small moment, Sarah was excited. She had liked James for as long as she could remember. But too much had happened in the last week, and she soon realized that she didn't care as much anymore. She was going to comment but her voice faded as they walked up toward the house. She was remembering seeing the person in her house while she drove off to the police station. Reminding herself that it was daylight, she was with friends, and that person likely wasn't in the house anymore, she had the courage to open the door with her house keys.

"Oh, my goodness, look at this mess!" Sarah shouted. The house had been ransacked. Fear gripped her heart and her imagination started sprinting in all sorts of directions.

Stina gasped. "Sarah, are you sure you want to be here, knowing that someone has been in here—or maybe still is?"

"I hate this." Sarah felt lost. She wandered through the living room and noticed all the turned-over furniture and the broken plates in the kitchen. "It's like nothing belongs to my family anymore. Who did this?"

She stood still, unable to process what she was seeing. Her eyes took note of the papers on the floor and the opened drawers. Things of value were still present, like the TV and kitchen blender. It was like someone was looking for something.

"Oh man, if we had known your house was like this, we would have called you—or called the police," Stina noted. "My parents keep a look out over your place and I don't think they've ever seen anyone suspicious hanging around." She paused. "Although, some lady parked out front once and went in, but my parents said that it was your social worker, or someone dealing with your dad's situation."

Stina grabbed her phone. "Maybe we should call the police now. Do you want me to?"

Leif answered, "You may not want to do that."

Stina gave him a confused look.

Sarah looked at her. "Don't call anyone. Everything that is going on is bigger than all of that right now. I have a chance to get my dad out of jail, so we need to focus on that! I'm sorry we even stopped here. Leif, let's just go to the pawn-shop and find the necklace and give it to your dad, and then your dad can help mine."

"How will a necklace help him?" Stina asked. "The pawn-shop you want to go to isn't the one where he got arrested, is it?"

Sarah didn't answer. Stina's eyes widened. "Really, you're wanting to go back in there?"

They slowly looked around the house and walked care-fully through all the broken things. Sarah peered out the window and saw Anthony smoking beside the car, seemingly oblivious.

"Well, let's get out of here," Leif said.

"Wait—I wanted to take another look for my journal. I left it upstairs in my room. Last time I was here, I couldn't find it." They followed Sarah up the stairs. Nothing seemed to be out of place in the bedrooms upstairs. It was like whoever decided to overturn her home had bypassed the second floor.

They walked back downstairs and into the living room. Leif and Stina started out the door. "Are you coming?" Stina called back.

"Yeah, I'll meet you out there," Sarah whispered and looked to the right, towards the window at the front of her house. There was a speckle of light. She felt like she was walking in a thick fog, but the air appeared as usual around her. It was how she felt when she was in the forests, when she'd see the sparkly lights. It was how she felt when she saw the leaf with the eye looking out. It was as if time had stopped and something or someone was making her focus her attention on the speckle of light. And there it was—the third key. Just sitting there on the windowsill, waiting for her to claim it. The words *protect the keys* echoed in her mind. She remembered the responsibility she felt for the other keys, but it was all too much to carry—especially when the reason for the keys was not clear. But for the first time, she felt regret that she had given the first two keys to Henrikson. The picture of the woman's hand holding out three keys flashed through her mind. She picked it up and the heaviness within the air disappeared. She was about to call for Leif to come and see the key but she decided against it. Henrikson already had two of the keys. She'd keep this one. Until all was understood, she would hang on to it.

Leif turned back into the living room, "Sarah? Are you OK?"

"Yeah, yeah." She smiled. "Let's go."

They all walked out of the house. Leif was watching Sarah intently, like he knew that something had happened.

Sarah looked at her phone. "What does Karen want?" she said. "Two missed calls from her."

"Does Karen know that you are here?" Stina asked. "What is going on?"

Sarah looked at Leif; she struggled to find the right words to explain to Stina. "She knows...but it's fine because I'm with my aunt traveling."

"I don't know what's going on here, but please don't go to that pawnshop," Stina continued, her voice serious. "It's not safe. Why put yourself through that? That's where your dad got arrested!"

Sarah interrupted. "I have to help him, Stina. Leif's dad promised to get my dad out of jail if I can get this necklace for him."

"Tell someone else to get the necklace for you!" Stina suggested.

"It's more complicated than that. I'm the only one who can get this necklace." Sarah shared.

Stina shook her head and continued down the sidewalk, "So, Leif, is your dad a judge or something?"

"No—but he is kind of like a lawyer and has the power to do that sort of stuff," he said as he looked at Anthony. "Let's move on to the pawnshop."

"No problem, sir," he said quickly. "Your father is almost in the city and will meet you there."

Stina raised her eyebrows and gave Sarah a look. "Sir?" She looked back at the house. "Hey look, there's something in your mailbox."

The mailbox for Sarah's house was at the top of their driveway. Sarah hadn't thought to look in it, but Stina was right, there was a small envelope sticking out of the box.

"My parents have been collecting your mail ever since your dad"—she paused—"left."

Sarah looked up at her and smiled gratefully.

"But it's been empty for the last few days. Until now," Stina finished.

Sarah walked slowly to the front of the house and took the envelope out of the box. It had the name *"Silver"* on it. She swallowed, suddenly feeling a rush of worry and excitement all at once. She had a flashback to when strangers had called her Silver. It made no sense at all. She held onto it tightly, not revealing the name on the envelope to Stina or Leif.

She looked over the forest. The glowing sparkles could be seen once again, quick to arrive, and quick to disappear. Nothing had changed. Leif's dad was the only person who made sense, even though the whole idea of stardust being important seemed crazy. It still felt fake—like she wasn't getting a full picture of the truth—but she didn't know what else to do. She felt the key in her zipped-up pocket. Perhaps she should just give it over, especially if there was a chance to get her dad out of jail.

CHAPTER 18

Anthony let them out in front of a pizza place near the pawnshop. It had been a long drive and none of them had eaten. He waited by the car while they went inside.

"Sarah, you've got to explain some things to me here." Stina was trying to make sense of everything.

Sarah felt bad that Stina was left in the dark, but how could she explain it to her without everything sounding crazy? They stood in line and received their steaming hot pizza. Sarah felt too bombarded with thoughts to be interested in eating. She knew she needed the food, though. She took a bite and the taste of the pizza quickly reminded her how hungry she was, and she devoured it.

Stina continued, "Why do you have a driver?" She looked back at Anthony. "You guys must be really rich or something."

"My dad owns a very large research company," Leif said.

Stina nodded cautiously. "Researching what?"

Leif took another bite of pizza before answering. "Geological stuff. He works with mining companies all around the world."

"Gold and diamonds?" Stina asked.

"Yes, and a substance even more valuable than that," Leif said, looking at Sarah. Sarah knew that he was talking about stardust and seafaen, something she was still learning about —and Stina had no clue.

She changed the subject. "OK, I'm going to go and see if this necklace is where my dad thinks it is." Sarah turned to Stina. "You don't have to come if you don't want to. I know all of this is crazy."

Stina looked unsure and worried. She looked at her phone. "I'll help you if you need it. Just explain it to me. What is happening?"

Sarah was about to start explaining but Leif interrupted.

"Did your dad say where in the pawnshop it would be specifically?" he asked. "Only you will be able to see it, Sarah."

"OK," Sarah replied, feeling brave. For once, her skill for seeing things that others could not was coming in handy. "I don't know where it is in the shop, exactly, but if it's there, I'll recognize it."

"You still haven't read the letter. What does it say?" Leif asked.

She nervously opened the crinkled envelope and looked down at it.

"It says …" Sarah started. She left out the words *For Silver* at the top. "*I think the necklace is still in the shop. It's important. It will help solve your problems.*" Sarah read it out loud, completely confused. "*I keep seeing vivid flashes of the necklace and I see the face now—the face of the woman who wore it. I think the necklace belonged to your mother. And I see her face and she looks so much like you. I must go but I hope this gets to you. If you meet a man named Viggo, he will give you the answers. Another thing. I Remember. Don't trust anyone who wants what you have.*

-Love from Dad."

Stina and Leif stared at her blankly.

"A man named Viggo?" Leif said. "Do you know him?"

"No. I don't know why my dad would tell me all of this, and I don't know what it means. I thought that my mother left. She left us." Sarah's voice shook. "It makes no sense." She looked at Leif.

"I'm sorry," Leif replied.

Stina saw the top of the letter, "Why does it say 'Silver' at the top?"

"I don't know," Sarah said. "Leif, this is why I was telling your dad that my dad might know something."

"Yeah. We should show him the letter," Leif said. Sarah noticed that he looked conflicted.

"Start from the beginning for me. Why are you so focused on going to the pawnshop and who are all these people that you are with … and why is this necklace so great?" Stina impatiently asked.

Sarah made her best effort to explain things to Stina, intentionally keeping out anything to do with the Startrail. Stina followed along, quietly listening.

"One second, my dad's calling." Leif got up suddenly and stepped outside the pizza shop.

"Who is this guy?" Stina asked. "How is it that we drove in a limo over here?"

"I don't know a lot about him other than that he was new to Walton, too. We became friends and he's been there for me, through all the crazy stuff."

"I am freaked out a little," Stina said. "He said only you would be able to see the necklace? Do you have special powers or something?" She laughed.

Sarah looked at her. "Remember when I told you I could see the sparkles in the forest and you just thought it was my imagination?"

"Yeah …" Stina reflected.

"Stina. I have some sort of"—she couldn't find the words —"some sort of ability."

"Ability to do what?"

"To see stuff, to see things that others cannot. It's hard to explain. I don't think you'll get it just yet."

Stina was about to take another bite of pizza but refrained and looked around. "OK, so, you do have super-powers." She laughed again. "Now, tell me the real story. You obviously can't be serious."

"See, I knew you wouldn't get it."

Stina placed the pizza on her paper plate. Her face looked puzzled, and yet it held interest in all that Sarah was saying. "You know, when we were kids and you told me that, I didn't know what to do with it, I just thought that you were being silly."

"Yeah, well, it is what it is. My own family didn't believe me, no one did, so it's not your fault. It's just that, all of a sudden, my world is starting to make sense, in a way I would have never expected."

"I may not understand, but you're my friend and I know things have been tough for you." Stina was trying to be sympathetic. "This Leif guy, he seems cool, but do you think you can trust him?"

Sarah was about to take the last bite of her pizza. "Why wouldn't I?"

"I don't know," Stina continued. "Forget what I said. Just, with everything going on, it just seems so crazy that these people drove you here and they are so willing to help you." She shrugged and continued eating. "Like, why are they so motivated?"

Sarah watched Leif talking on the phone outside the window. Anthony was leaning against the vehicle, watching Leif, too. He caught Leif's attention and pointed at his watch.

She watched him talking. He was pacing the sidewalk, speaking into his phone with emotion. Suddenly a new perspective about Leif came trampling into her mind. Not to mention the questions that arose from the letter that her dad had written to her. Was it really meant for her? Who was Silver? She needed to ask Grandfather, wherever he was. He would know.

"I think they need me to help them somehow. And I think I want to, especially if there is a chance that they can get my dad out of jail," Sarah said. "Let's go. I promise I'll explain everything to you after we get the necklace."

They left the pizza place and joined Leif outside.

"All I am saying is that I don't think it's fair, Dad. It's cruel." Leif's voice went from a shout to a whisper as he saw Sarah approaching him. "I've got to go. I'll call you later." He ended his call and smiled at Sarah. Her heart flipped. His brown eyes met hers. "Are you OK?"

"Yeah, I'm fine." She smiled slightly. Her hand held the key in her pocket. At this point it would make sense to just hand over the third key, but she hesitated.

Anthony watched with careful eyes from a distance.

"Are you OK?" Sarah asked, "It looks like you were having an intense conversation."

"I wish things were different, I wish that you knew more about all of this." Leif shifted where he stood and looked at the sidewalk, and then brought his gaze back to Sarah. "Remember how I told you that my dad and I aren't that close?"

"Yeah," Sarah replied.

"Well, he keeps me in the dark on a lot of stuff. This trip here, this mission, it was a way to get closer to him, to spend time with him." He looked up and then back at Sarah. "I just don't agree with some of the stuff he's involved in."

"Like what?"

"I'll try and tell you later, OK? Right now, Anthony is on

my case and so is my father. They are meeting us at the pawnshop."

"Does it have to do with me?" Sarah looked up into his eyes. The wind blew his hair slightly.

"Yeah, it does. I didn't think that I would …" Leif paused. "Like you. Like I do." He took her hand and looked into her eyes. "I came here for a job, I came here for the Startrail mission. But there's something that my dad isn't telling us, I know it. Something he won't admit to. And I'm conflicted." Leif breathed in and let go of Sarah's hand. "Come on, let's go into the pawnshop. It's closing soon." He motioned toward the sign with the hours. He looked back at Anthony. "Just know that I've realized that I don't know everything that my dad knows about this, and—I'm sorry if he does anything crazy."

"What would he do?" she asked, her mind going in a million directions.

"I don't know," he said quietly.

Dark clouds were moving in fast and began to cover the sunny sky. Cars were whooshing by as they walked toward the pawnshop. An angry customer pushed the door open in a huff. "A bunch of garbage, that's all it is!" he yelled as he stormed past Sarah and Leif, disrupting their conversation.

Leif's brown eyes glistened and a lock of hair fell over them. "Just know, I'm on your side. Let's just get this necklace and then we will go from there."

"Do you really think your dad will help my dad?"

"I hope so," Leif said.

"After I get this necklace for you, and get my dad out of jail, I'm out of here. I need to get back to my regular life."

"Regular life?" Leif moved closer to her. "You are anything but regular. Why is it that people from Earth Realm want their regular lives, when the true reality is so much greater?"

She turned and opened the pawnshop door. "I don't have

the luxury of knowing any more about the Startrail than what I've learned since last night. I still feel confused by the loss of my memory, from when I was young. Total understanding of this new reality isn't easy for me. I'm sorry." Tears were beginning to brim, accompanied by a faint migraine. "Let's just get this over with."

Anthony called Leif over to the vehicle. "I'll meet you two in there," Leif said. He backed up and spun around, walking towards Anthony.

Stina and Sarah walked in and the door slammed shut. Stina looked around and then over at Sarah. "Are you OK?"

Sarah felt uneasy knowing that this was where her father got into trouble, but she was determined to get the necklace.

"I'm fine. I just hate this. The last few weeks have been so confusing, and so mind-opening." Her eyes were filled with tears. "But all that I think about is my dad in jail. It hurts knowing that he is in a cell all alone. He's all I have. I can't be stupid anymore, I need to help him."

"I'm sorry," Stina said. "You've gone through so much." She tried to focus on the situation. "OK. We're here now. What are we looking for?"

Sarah looked back outside. Leif was leaning into the passenger's window talking to Anthony.

"I really need to see if I can find this necklace. I've brought some money with me and maybe I can get it, show my dad, and give it to his lawyer to help his case. No one else is helping him. I don't even know where Grandpa is. So I have to do it!" Determined, she scoured the store to find the jewelry.

"Let's do this!" Stina shrugged and followed her through the dimly lit shop. There were tons of antiques all over the place. Old clocks lined one of the walls; guitars and old paintings were on the back wall.

Stina looked at some racks of vintage clothing. "Whoa,

these are interesting dresses," she observed. She picked up a velvet black hat and placed it on her head.

Behind the glass by the counter, Sarah spotted the jewelry, but she couldn't see anything special. There was a variety of jewelry available. Some antique, some modern. There were a few lockets on display, some were heart-shaped, others oval. The reddish jeweled necklace from the picture wasn't to be found. She pulled the picture out of her pocket and looked at it again before searching through the options.

Sarah couldn't see any of the staff anywhere, but she noticed that the door was open to the back room. The hard-wood floor creaked beneath their feet.

She heard some steps shuffling around in the back room. Stina was still looking through old clothes behind her. While she waited, suddenly one necklace caught her eye. It was silver and it had an oval shape. There were carvings behind the gemstone, and it was the same shape and ruby color as in the picture. *That could be it*, she considered. It was in the cabinet, in a separate wooden box that had glass on the top. All she needed to do was flip the necklace over and see if the three keys were on it.

Finally, someone came out of the back room. It was an old man with white hair. He was wearing a suit and had glasses on, and he was upset at being disturbed. "What can I help you with?" he asked.

Sarah quickly came up with an idea, "I'm looking for a vintage necklace to buy my"—she was trying to think of who she could be buying the gift for—"my aunt."

"Well, they are all in front of you, so pick whichever one you'd like," the man said.

"I keep looking at the one in the wooden case. The red-jeweled one with the carvings behind the gem. Can I see what is on the back of it? How much would that one be?"

It was a longshot that it was the one her father was looking for. Maybe that one was hidden away, or maybe it had never been here to begin with.

"I don't know what you mean, the one with the jewel and carvings? There isn't one like that, nor is there a wooden case." The man looked at her with piercing eyes. "Where do you see it?"

"That one right th—" Before finishing her sentence, Sarah realized that she was the only one who could see the necklace. No one else. That had to make it the right necklace. She felt a sense of pride that she was able to see it, but not the others. This is what they'd expected of her.

Sarah could feel something moving in her jacket pocket. She reached in and realized the key was floating within the small confines. She remembered Gale saying how the power of stardust could make things do amazing things. The key was sensing it. She tried to focus as she reflected. The man looked at her strangely and started walking backwards.

He picked up the phone and started dialing, his eyes still on Sarah. Then he took the phone to the back room.

Stina gave Sarah a blank stare.

"I don't see anything like what you described," Stina said. "Which necklace do you mean?"

The door to the pawnshop opened and shut.

"Did you find it?" Leif said, suddenly showing up behind them.

"Leif." Her heart leapt at the sight of him. She thought of the letter. What her father had said—don't trust anyone. What did he mean by that?

"I think we should get out of here. Sarah, take the necklace and run."

If no one else could see it, then she should just take it, she reasoned. She thought about how to go about that. It was in the cabinet; she'd have to go behind the counter to retrieve it.

"How can I explain to someone that I need to take an invisible necklace?" Sarah whispered in frustration. Leif looked antsy and continued to watch the door.

"Invisible necklace?" Stina said slowly. "You guys are freaking me out."

Sarah looked in her pocket and saw that the key was still floating. She zipped up the pocket and walked to the corner where all the books were displayed. No one else could see her there. She unzipped her pocket again and held the key in her hands. The pressure of it rising was startling. Her mind was racing. The key stopped forcing upwards and rested on her hand. Then it started floating and moving forward, through the aisles of books. She kept her hands cupped around it as it propelled forward. She looked around and could see Stina and Leif walking across the store toward her.

"Sarah, what are you doing? What is that?" Stina could see her following something and she eventually saw the key afloat, just above her hands.

Sarah let the key move a little more freely. As it floated from her hand, it continued down the aisle quickly and steadily, only to suddenly stop above an old dresser. She grabbed it and quickly stuffed it back into her pocket. She turned to Stina. "Did you see that?"

Stina just stood looking at the dresser. "I saw."

"Sarah, is that the other …" The door opened again. Leif's dad had arrived.

Sarah unzipped her jacket pocket and the key floated out and hovered in front of her once again.

"Sarah. Leif." Henrikson walked toward them. "You don't say. You found the other one."

She knew that the key would not leave her side until Leif's dad put the coating on it like he had with the others. Now she had a reason to want to keep it for herself. *Don't trust anyone who wants what you have,* her father's letter told her. Did he mean the keys?

Henrikson walked over as if to take the key. Sarah stepped back.

"OK, then. Listen, I'm only here to help," Henrikson said.

Stepping back to avoid him, she walked into an old lamp which fell to the ground and smashed all over the place.

"Put it back in your pocket and let's go!" Stina whispered forcefully.

Henriksen's eyes followed the key as Sarah placed it back into her pocket.

"This is Leif's dad," Sarah shared with Stina.

"Sarah, this is where you said that the necklace would be. Any luck in finding it?" he asked.

"Well, yes, I ..." Sarah still could see what Leif and Stina couldn't, and probably everyone else. "I don't know."

"Well, let's find it." Henrikson spun around and walked toward the cabinets. He motioned with his hand toward the necklaces. "Mr. Garrison, please let her take whatever she wants."

Henrikson was speaking to the white-haired man, Mr. Garrison. It sounded like they knew each other. Something wasn't adding up. Why would Leif's dad know the pawnshop keeper? And if Mr. Garrison was at the pawnshop when her dad was set up for the crime he didn't commit, then he would know the truth. For the first time, it was apparent that Henrikson might know more about her dad's situation than he let on.

CHAPTER 19

The dim lights in the pawn shop flickered.

Mr. Garrison nodded at Henrikson. "Sir, you said this time would come and now it is here. You must be so pleased."

"How do you know this man?" Sarah jumped in. She felt her voice shake. She was nervous, it was all too strange and too planned.

"I work with Henrikson," Garrison confirmed.

"Well then, you must know that my father is innocent right?" The words shot out of Sarah's mouth. She had to ask. "You must have been here that night."

Garrison looked at Henrikson.

"Right? I mean, you guys can help him. My father," Sarah said. "You said you would help him if I get you the necklace."

"Yes, we will help your father, Sarah. But we need the necklace to do so," Henrikson said in a calm voice. "Go ahead, take the necklace, and let's go. We will stay in Augusta tonight. We have a place for you." He paused. "It'll all work out."

Sarah could feel the key in her jacket pocket. It wasn't

moving now. She looked around at everyone waiting for her to make the next move. Leif stood behind his dad; he looked conflicted.

It would be the simplest thing for her to get the necklace and follow Henrikson, but her dad's note said not to trust anyone. She heard movement ahead of her in the back corner of the pawnshop. To her surprise, she saw that Ivo, the long-haired man from Walton, was there once again. How did he know that they were here? Was he following them?

"You!" Sarah backed away. "How did you get here? Get away!"

"The back door." He motioned towards the door that opened onto an alleyway. "Let me explain, I didn't get a chance to before. I didn't know. I didn't understand." The long haired man tried to reason as he confidently moved toward her. "My name is Ivo. I've been sent to help you."

"Help me? Why does everyone want to help me? It makes no sense. What do you want?" Sarah shouted. Her head felt like it was on a swivel looking back and forth from Ivo to Henrikson and Garrison. "Do you want the keys too?"

Stina grabbed an antique book and held it up like a weapon, towards Ivo. "Sarah, let's go!" Stina shouted.

Ivo tried not to laugh. "Really? A book? You must trust me —I can help you get away out the back."

"Get away from what?" Sarah continued to back away and Stina held the book even higher. Stina had her other hand on her phone ready to call for help if necessary.

"If you go out the front, your social worker will be waiting for you," he said. Sarah looked confused, why would Karen be outside? How did she know that she was here? "But if you come with me, I might be able to give you some answers."

"Believe him, Sarah." Tindra appeared in the back door-way, behind Ivo. "I know I do."

"Tindra!" A sense of relief came over Sarah. "How did you get here?"

Henrikson moved closer. "Ivo, stay away from her. These are matters that do not concern you."

"They concern me very well," Ivo's voice growled back.

A thick, large man came into view from behind Garrison. He was around seven feet tall, dressed professionally, and with long, greying black hair, tied back. His eyes were coal black, just like the men back in Walton who had jumped out and tried to grab her and Tindra.

"You have found the necklace. The plan worked. We have been looking for you. Waiting for you." The giant man spoke carefully, watching Sarah intently.

Then he stood tall and silent, his eyes on Ivo, then Sarah. He stepped closer to them.

Sarah noted that Ivo was getting restless.

"No one is in trouble," the large man said. "We just need Sarah to give us the necklace." His voice was deep; every step he took was heavy on the tiled floor. He cracked his ruddy knuckles.

Sarah backed up nervously. "Why does everyone care about the necklace? We just want to get out of here, OK?" She looked at her friends who were watching her intently.

Sarah tried to run to the front door. The man blocked her in the book aisle.

"Your father tried to do what you're doing and take the necklace for himself. You don't want the same thing to happen to you, do you?" The man laughed.

"Not now, Cody," Henrikson ordered.

Leif stepped forward. "Dad, what's going on here?"

"Stina, call the cops," Sarah urged.

Cody glared at Stina, then faced Sarah again, unfazed by

the threat of cops. He laughed. "This is well beyond stuff that cops deal with. Looks like you're going to be staying here with us."

Henrikson was now facing the cabinets, scouring each corner, "Garrison, take all of it. If she won't tell us where it is, we will take all of it."

Garrison followed instructions and started to push all of the necklaces into a large canvas bag.

"You think you will take something that has been hidden by a Portal Painter?" Ivo scoffed.

Henrikson looked at Ivo briefly but nodded for Garrison to continue collecting the jewelry.

Sarah was conflicted and her headache was getting worse. Leif walked up to her. His eyes bored into Cody as he stood next to her, then he focused on Sarah.

"Sarah, show us where the necklace is. The necklace is powerful. It can help people travel through seafaen walls and regular man-made walls. It will help get your dad out." He paused and looked over at Ivo, then walked closer to her. "What's the hesitation?"

"Leif, did you know about this? He just said that my dad tried to do what I am doing? You mean, they knew what was going on that night?" Her voice started to shake, "They knew that he'd go to jail?"

"Cody doesn't know what he is talking about, Sarah." Henrikson tried to reason with her. "He knew about your father, but it was out of our control that he went to jail. Now, we can go get him out of jail if you cooperate. We have taken all that we could take from where you say the necklace was hidden. Last chance to tell us where it is."

Leif had confusion written all over his face. The words from her father were clear, that she should trust no one. But her father wanted the necklace and so did Henrikson. And it was either for the same reason or very different ones.

"Sarah come with us." Ivo motioned with his head for her to follow him. Tindra stood behind him.

"Come along now, Sarah, listen to Henrikson," urged Cody.

Sarah searched Cody's face. Confusion took over and her painful headache resumed. She caught a glimpse of what looked like a gun inside Cody's jacket. His black eyes flashed, reminding her of the men that came out of nowhere in Walton and lifted Tindra up by the arm. They, too, had the black eyes, and for some reason they had the power to make her extremely weak.

She backed away from him. Catching his eyes quickly with hers, she felt a surge of power go out from her. Cody smirked. She forced her head to turn away. Maybe the necklace would have to wait. Maybe she needed to get as far away as possible from these people who wanted things from her.

"You know about what happened to my father. You know why he is in jail, don't you …" Sarah felt anger rushing through her blood with all this new information about her father and the thought that they might have had something to do with his arrest.

Ivo jumped in. "I think it's time you trusted me." She turned to look at him.

"You're going to trust that man who's been following you around? Over someone who knows that your father is innocent. Who can eventually help his case?" Henrikson reasoned with an unusually calm voice. "This prison is only temporary. He will get out. We will get him out. Come on, Sarah, your aunt is waiting for us."

"Sarah. Come with us." Ivo was at the back door. Tindra was still behind him.

She was so close to the necklace, so close. If she just ran up to get it and then left with Ivo, that would solve everything. She took the chance and ran past Cody and behind the cabinets. Cody was about to stop her but Henrikson motioned for him to hold back.

"Let her retrieve it first," he shouted.

Her heart was pounding. It was all too simple, yet if she made the wrong move maybe the necklace would be in the wrong hands. She was behind the cabinets now and they all were watching quietly, waiting for her to take this special item.

Ivo was moving closer. "If you see it, don't take it. Not now. Trust me, you don't want the enemy to have that kind of power."

The enemy. Who really was the enemy? Her headache was getting stronger, she was confused, but the anchor was the note that her father had sent her.

Sarah decided it was better to at least get out of the building and follow Ivo. If Tindra trusted him, then she could too. But her heart sank. She didn't have the necklace. The necklace sparkled, sitting in the cabinet, unseen by the rest of the world.

She slowly backed away from the cabinets, making her decision. She spun around and rushed for the door, the man with black eyes lurched forward and grabbed Sarah's arm.

"Let me go!" she shouted, pulling away from him.

"You must get the necklace. Now!" the man said.

Garrison grabbed Sarah by the other arm. "Get the necklace and let's go," he commanded.

Sarah struggled to get out of his grip. Ivo ran toward her as she was being dragged back toward the jewelry cabinet.

"Take it and let's go," Garrison repeated.

"Let her go!" Leif shouted, "What are you guys doing? This is Sarah here. Back off!"

He ran up and started pulling Garrison away from Sarah.

"Leif?" Sarah said, her voice in almost a whisper. "My dad is in jail because of these people."

"Trust me—I'm sure it's not like that." Leif looked at his father, desperation in his eyes.

"Why didn't you say anything? How could you ...?" Her voice faltered.

"I never knew that was what happened, not until now. You've got to believe me, Sarah," Leif pleaded.

The black-eyed man had her arms pinned behind her back.

"Let her go!" Ivo shouted from the top of the aisle.

"Or what? My orders are my orders and you know who I work for, so you better back off." Cody's hands turned into fists, and one of them slowly reached inside his jacket for the gun .

"You must have forgotten that the powers that I hold have been around for much longer than yours. You don't scare me." Ivo brought his hand up and held it in front of Sarah and her captor.

The man laughed at the sight. "That won't work here. Earth is a place without that kind of magic."

Sarah struggled to get free. Ivo's hand was steady.

"Leif—make her get that necklace so we can get out of here," Henrikson demanded.

"I will not make her do anything," Leif said. Sarah could tell he was conflicted about the whole situation.

"It's not up to you. You have your orders. You took your oath," Henrikson spewed.

Sarah remembered Leif trying to explain the oath. She felt a slight moment of sympathy for him. But how could he be involved in something that sent her father to jail? She hated that he was involved in it; it was hard for her to even look at him. He wasn't who she thought he was.

Ivo's hand was still in the air.

Cody covered his eyes with one hand and began to cower slightly at whatever power was coming from Ivo. The grip around Sarah's arm became loose and she pulled herself away. Her eyes widened as she realized what was happening. She began walking backwards toward Ivo, speechless at the sight. The man who had tried to take her was completely frozen in time.

"What did you do?" Henrikson's eyes widened in disbelief. "There's no need to use power like that, Ivo."

"You leave me no choice when you are putting the future Keeper in danger," Ivo said with confidence.

"How dare you?" Henrikson's voice became dark, brimming with anger. "You seem sure of yourself now, but with time you'll see. You'll see that you will need us." His fists clenched. "You Erleonians are nothing without the United Ones. NOTHING!"

The lights flickered in the pawnshop making it hard to see for a moment.

Sarah was now standing behind Ivo, and he was guiding her out of the shop while his hand was still raised toward Henrikson and Leif. He was creating a force that kept them at bay.

Leif tried to walk toward them but couldn't. "Sarah, please. Please work with us here."

"Don't let her get away, Leif!" Henrikson shouted, struggling against the powerful force directed towards him.

Sarah looked directly into his eyes. "He already did."

Leif pulled his hand through his hair. "Sarah. Please." The force from Ivo was like a wind moving him backwards, he crouched down.

Henrikson made one last unsuccessful effort to run towards Sarah and Ivo. "We know you have it, the third key, but we have the others. Not to mention the greatest weapon that the Startrail has ever seen." His voice strained. "This is not over!"

Leif ran after his father and grabbed his arm, causing him

to stop. He immediately turned towards Leif. "You let her go." He paused, speechless with anger. "It's not just the necklace. It's the other key that we still need, Leif. This isn't just about you and some girl."

Ivo lifted his arm again towards the cabinets and immediately they shattered into a thousand pieces of glass all around the shop. Everyone turned their heads and covered their eyes.

Leif let go of his father's arm and crouched down while the dust from the shattered glass cabinets settled to the floor. His hand covered his face, defeated. Sarah's heart sank, seeing Leif in conflict, but she knew that she had made the right decision to go with Ivo. There was so much yet to understand.

Henrikson turned and ran out the front door, leaving Leif behind.

"Anthony, follow them!" he shouted. "They're around the back!"

Ivo led Sarah through the back door and into the alley where Tindra and Stina were waiting for them in a black vehicle. Tindra was trying to fill Stina in with the information about the keys.

CHAPTER 20

The evening air was crisp and it was already dark; the moon struggled to reveal itself through the overcast sky.

Ivo jumped into the driver's seat, started the car, and screeched down the alleyway. Sarah sunk back in the seat, closed her eyes, and then took out her phone.

Leif: I am sorry for what happened. I have so much to tell you.

Sirens were sounding and tires screeched around the corner, stopping in front of the pawnshop. Sarah looked to the left and saw the road that led to the trails that she used to run through. They eventually led to her old neighborhood. Sarah's heart was beating faster. The realization of what just took place was starting to settle. The necklace existed. It was in the shop and only she could see it. They all wanted her to find it for them, but she no longer believed they wanted to help get her dad out of jail. They might even have helped put him there. And Ivo has crazy powers to freeze people. He must be trustworthy if Tindra was with him. This is all she knew for now. And then there was Leif. Was he just pretending to be her friend? As a means to an end?

The keys.

The stupid keys. A part of her wanted to rush back and give them the third key and be done with it. But maybe she had it all wrong. She could easily be rid of all the keys, but would they let her go?

"Keep driving. We gotta get away. I can't show my face to the police. I don't want to make anything worse for my dad," Sarah shouted.

Ivo drove on, his long hair blowing out of the open window. Sarah had the key in her pocket. It was still warm, which made her nervous. She looked in the pocket, it was glowing, and once again it started to float.

"Guys. It's doing it again. It's starting to float," Sarah shouted. "You have to pull over."

To her right was the ravine, with woods that had trails leading all around the city, leading out to her neighborhood.

"What do you mean?" Ivo said, still driving at top speed. "Listen, those keys are extremely powerful, so my gut says that we need to get them to Mildred immediately-even if it's just the one. She'll know how to deal with it."

"Who?" Sarah said frantically. "Where is she? Why will she know?"

"In Norway," Ivo said. "For now, we will have to take you back to Walton, figure out a way to get the other keys back. Then we take them to Norway. Mildred is in a safe place, a place completely hidden from the world."

"Where in Norway?" Tindra asked.

Before Ivo could respond, Sarah interrupted.

"I need you to pull over!" Sarah felt like she was lifting along with the key. Her head hit the roof of the car.

"Whoa, Sarah! What's happening!?" Stina shouted. The car began to rise slightly before dropping onto the road again, the tires screeching.

"Please pull over. We are far enough out. I can always run

into the woods for cover." Ivo looked in the mirrors. No cars were following him anymore. At least for now. The power of the key was continuous; it was getting more forceful.

"Don't touch me. Or you'll lift too." They didn't do anything. Ivo pulled over; the back of the car continued to lift upwards with the force of the key.

"What is happening?" shrieked Stina.

"Open the door. The keys have minds of their own, it seems," Sarah said. Stina followed orders and opened the door, just as the back of the car came crashing down again. "I'm sorry. I'm sorry you guys." Sarah felt bad, she felt responsible for getting her friends into this mess.

She fell out of the car, still semi-floating. The key continued to move forward and then it fell into the frosted grass. Sarah was able to let go of it.

A moment later it rose and started floating forward again, just in front of Sarah. She followed it.

"Sarah, we will help you." Ivo chased after her. Stina and Tindra watched from behind.

Sirens could be heard in the distance.

"Ivo, your car. We need to get out of here," Tindra said.

Ivo looked conflicted. He saw Sarah running into the woods, then looked at Tindra and Stina. "Where do these paths lead?"

"They lead to Sarah's neighborhood. We used to run these trails all the time," Stina explained, her voice shaky. "What about Sarah?"

"Sarah's resourceful, the key couldn't be in safer hands," Ivo said. "I'll follow her and make sure she's OK. Tindra, you take the keys to the car and drive out of here. Go somewhere safe." He nodded at her. She grabbed the keys warily. Sarah was just about to enter the woods, with the key leading her forward.

CHAPTER 21

She felt a deep sense of urgency to get out of sight. Ivo was running towards her. She wanted to trust him because Tindra did, but she still hadn't made up her own mind as to who was telling the truth. The police lights could be seen on the street outside the trail. The cars had stopped. She was only twenty yards into the darkened trail and she decided to pick up her pace.

Ivo was now running after her, to catch up, and get away. "Sarah. The key. People are going to be coming after you now because of this key. There is more to this world that you may not understand. It will seem strange. But promise me, you must protect the key. Do not give it to anyone."

"It's moving faster and faster. It's like it's leading me somewhere," Sarah shouted in the darkness.

"Don't stop! They are coming!" Ivo shouted, trying to keep pace. "There is more to your story than what you know, than what you remember."

Than what I remember. She thought about what had happened before the accident. There had to be more. More to her identity. She could see the path beneath her feet, lit by the crescent moon. She knew these trails well; she knew that eventually she would reach her own neighborhood. Her heart was pounding, and her head soon followed suit; her headache was coming back. *Please, no, not now.*

The key was still illuminated and hovering in front of her. But it suddenly stopped and dropped in the center of the path. A creature scurried among the snowy trees behind her. Everything went silent.

"Who's there? … Ivo?" she shouted. There was no answer. The darkness seemed to be caving in on her.

The crazy rush of getting out of the car with the key and following it while the police chased them all came to a sudden halt.

"Ivo?" She called for him one more time. He must have decided to turn around. Or maybe Sarah had taken a different trail than the one she was used to, one with more turns and multiple options. She stopped running when she reached the key, and felt for her phone in her pocket. As she found it, she saw that the key was starting to light up and glow again. Her headache began again, but then stopped right away. She didn't understand. She looked down the path behind her and tried to listen for footsteps.

"You obviously want me to take care of you." She spoke to the key like it was her pet. A creature she had to take care of. "What is it that you want from me?" She bent down and picked it up again. She continued to walk briskly, expecting that the entrance to her street would be coming up. But the space around her was different. She didn't recognize it—it was as if it held a subtle glow. It was similar to the secret realm where the United Ones' headquarters was. There was still no sign of Ivo. He must have turned around, or maybe he couldn't get into the space, wherever she was. She still didn't understand the physics of it. She held the key in her hand and as it glowed, she noticed a shadow moving ahead of her. Her heart started to pound. "Ivo?" she shouted.

The shadow came into the light.

"Who are you?" Sarah turned to run.

"Wait. Wait! You … you said Ivo." The man's eyes were genuine. He had long hair that hadn't been combed in a while and his beard was unkempt. He was wearing a white dress shirt and black pants. He was carrying a bag with him. "Please—wait. I'm not going to hurt you."

"Who are you?"

"I'm Viggo."

Sarah stared at him. "The letter."

"How is it that you are able to enter this place?" Viggo asked.

"I don't know much about it. All I know is that I was on the trail to my house, but this place is … different." Her head started pounding. She walked backwards but tripped on a root sticking out of the ground.

The glowing key fell out of her hand. Viggo noticed it but didn't run for it. "I'm not going to hurt you," he said cautiously, eyes locked on the key, "but tell me if you know Ivo. He's … he's my son."

She picked up the key. "Yes, he was following me, but then he disappeared when I entered this place."

"Oh, this is good news. He told me his base was in a place called Walton, but you say he's here?" Viggo's eyes sparkled with joy.

"You might find him once you get back onto the path— the regular path."

"Thank you."

Sarah turned to walk away.

"Listen. I … I don't have much time, but I can't help but see that you have one of the missing keys."

"How do you know about the keys?"

"We both have found ourselves having entry into this secret space within Earth Realm. Of course I know about the keys. You see, I'm looking for a friend's daughter. His name is Stannach, well, he goes by Stanley Carlson here."

"That's my dad!" Sarah reached into her jean pocket and pulled out the note. She looked around, still expecting people to be following her. "I found this in my mailbox earlier today. It's a note that mentions you. It says that I should trust you." She reluctantly gave it over to Viggo.

Viggo's head fell back and he closed his eyes. "I knew it— the old boy is remembering. With the help of the fairies." The tone of his voice became serious again. "You must be Silver, then."

"I'm Sarah. But my dad addressed this note to Silver. Anyway, I need to get out of here. But do you think you're able to help my dad?"

"Yes, yes, that's why I came here. But the portals I arrived in are only active for so long. I will try and return when I can. All I know is that I can't be stuck here."

"Portals." Her heart started beating. They had told her that portals existed, and she had seen them at the United Ones' headquarters, but her head had a hard time truly believing this was happening. "Where do you come from?"

"Ordillaz. You must tell no one of our meeting. But I must say, if you are truly your father's daughter, then our meeting is not by accident. Not to mention how happy your mother would be to know …"

Voices were heard in the distance.

"My mother?"

"This way!" a man's voice shouted.

"Only the United Ones have access to this place right now. I only have access because I have something special with me." He looked at her seriously. "I don't know what happened to you and your father—losing your memories, I mean—but I think it was foul play."

That made sense to her, based on what she had heard from Cody.

Viggo continued, his hands on Sarah's shoulders. "You must listen to me. Protect this key, but also—take this."

He placed a leather satchel in her hands. "In it is seafaen. The ingredient …"

"The ingredient to paint portals." She finished his sentence and smiled slightly.

"You have a key. Where are the other keys?"

"Henrikson. He has them both."

"Henrikson." His eyes widened. "The United Ones. You must do everything you can to stay away from those liars. He brought her into the shelter of some nearby evergreens. There was a stony surface beneath them. "Hurry, we don't have much time. In my bag I have some paint, in that bag is seafaen. Please tell me you have a brush."

She felt startled but tried to remain focused on what was happening. She remembered putting the broken paintbrush into her bag after the gallery incident. Reaching into her bag her hand found it and she pulled it out.

"You are your mother's daughter."

Sarah felt proud in that moment, but she didn't know why just yet. The flash of the blue vase pouring out was suddenly intertwined with a new half of a vision, a bottle of paint was opened on a table and the blue vase was tipped and liquid poured out of it into the paint bottle. The vision made so much more sense now. Viggo took out some paint that he had with him and Sarah opened the satchel. The same sparkling substance that Henrikson had at the headquarters was inside. "I mix it with the paint?"

"Yes—we need to get you out of here."

"What about you?"

"There's a portal to Ordillaz waiting for me, and I only have enough to get me back there. Otherwise, I'm stuck here." He looked around anxiously. "They are coming. Paint something—paint what you know. And hide. Wherever you go, you will find people who will take care of you. Hang on to the key."

She looked up at him with confusion; she wished he would spell it out for her.

"Go on. Mix it together on this rock."

He found a piece of bark that was about the size of sticky-note paper and put it beside the rock.

Viggo provided her with two colors to use. Sarah mixed the substances together on the rock and then held the paintbrush in her hand. The mix sparkled gloriously and looked like miniature whirlpools on the rock. Her eyes widened as she remembered the power that came out of her at the gallery.

"You want me to paint something on the bark? With only two colors?" Her mouth went dry.

"If you paint it on the bark, I can take it with me safely." He nodded at her reassuringly. "Go on. Paint."

"I think I can hear them. There were agents with Henrikson that had crazy powers."

"Ignore it. Right now you need to focus on this one task. If Ivo is nearby, I know he can ward them off." He was breathing heavily and keeping watch while Sarah was crouched down over the piece of bark. "Go."

Sarah put down the color on the bark. The colors he provided were a deep shade of yellow and a dark green. She painted one streak and then another with the green; she made shapes like trees and the yellow color was like lights that she lightly added in among the green. It was definitely abstract. Just then she felt the power surge out of her arms and onto the bark.

"This is amazing," Viggo whispered under his breath. "You really are her."

She looked up briefly into Viggo's eyes before the power within her arm forced her like a magnet to keep painting. Immediately, the trees that she had painted started to move and the yellow dots within them started to glisten like lights. Her hand was shaking and sweat started pouring down her face. She smiled and dropped the paintbrush. "It's done."

Viggo then took a bottle of water and poured it over top of the rock that had the paint mixtures. "That'll get rid of some of the evidence, although there is still seafaen on that rock for those who can see it."

The voices were getting louder.

"You have painted yourself into a realm within this realm where you will encounter a good friend of mine."

"Wait—you know the place I painted?"

"Go. Find her. I cannot utter her name. These forests have ears and eyes everywhere. You'll know who she is—she'll find you."

"What do you mean, go?"

"You don't remember, do you? Just like your father. Your father and you used to travel a lot through portals, but for some reason you have forgotten. The deceit that has been going on is unfathomable. Something happened ten years ago, after the war, but it wasn't an accident, I can tell you that much." He looked back nervously. Then he smiled slightly. "It's fitting that you painted your way into this particular realm."

"What do you mean, it wasn't an accident? You mean, someone took our memories?" Sarah tried to grasp onto something that made sense.

"I don't know, I'm sorry. But, something tells me you will find out soon." Viggo shifted slightly. "This trip into Earth

Realm has been worthwhile in every sense of the word. Now, let's move on."

"Which realm did I paint?"

"The realm of fairies," Viggo said with conviction. "Once you enter in, I will keep this portal safe. The fairy I am speaking of will tell you where you must go next. But your main goal is to keep this one key safe. It is our only hope now that the other two keys are in *his* hands. It's up to you now."

"I don't understand."

Viggo rushed along. "If you see Ivo before I do, tell him that I have come—and that soon, once the Painter's Keep is back under the control of the Portal Painters, then I will see him. Tell him his mother and I are safe, and his sister too. Tell no one else that you have seen me."

"What about my mother?"

"You will know soon enough. Your mother is extremely powerful—but I think she may need our help."

They could hear the sound of something rustling in the trees.

"I see movement in there." A voice that sounded like Garrison reached them. "Sir, it looks like she's with someone."

"Sarah?" Gale's voice sounded.

For a moment, she considered running out to her aunt, and seeing Leif, and trying to see if she could gain under-standing—but there was no time. She had the gift of painting portals and her destiny was beyond the United Ones. At least, that was what Viggo was trying to say. And her father said that Viggo could be trusted.

"Dive in. Look at the painting and move toward it. It'll pull you in," Viggo said. "I will take it to Ordillaz with me and find another way to help, eventually. Remember what I told you. Farewell, Silver of Ocean Sky."

He smiled at her and Sarah held the painting in front of

her. It started moving faster, and like a magnetic pull, she was brought in, leaving the world behind her and hoping that Viggo was able to get away.

She immediately felt like she was falling down a warm tunnel of darkness and the pressure of the atmosphere felt extremely soft. She was able to open her eyes for a moment, but it was far too bright. Then it was as if time had stopped and she felt like she was floating in nothingness. She couldn't tell if her eyes were open or not, but she noticed a tiny flutter of wings going into a doorway in front of her. She felt her hand grasping the key. Within moments the nothingness turned into the pressure of liquid around her and all she could feel was her heartbeat and the heat from the key being squeezed in her hand. The liquid smelled like roses, pine, and chocolate. Her eyes were shut, and they felt heavy, but she struggled to open them with all her might. The smells immediately went away and her eyes became irritated by the atmosphere. She tried to breathe, but she couldn't. The air felt heavy, like weights, but she could still move in it. She finally realized that she was in water. A glow from the key beamed through the clear water and she could see light at the surface. She panicked and swam upwards and upwards— looking below only once to see a whirlpool of light closing beneath her. The portal back to her world lay at the bottom of a body of water.

The fact that she had just gone through a portal painting —that *she* had created—was too much to grasp. Her mind raced while she swam upwards, broke the water, and gasped for air.

The End

ABOUT THE AUTHOR

H.A. Stephen is an entrepreneur, athlete, and lover of castles. When she is not working on writing projects, she runs her bustling coffee shop, Apartment 3 Espresso Bar, dreams up new ideas with her husband, and runs on nearby tracks. Previously, she has represented Canada on the Bobsleigh World Cup circuit and has gathered much fuel for her imagination and writing from her travels. Follow her @heatherannstephen.